LOVE BOMB

PENNY KNIGHT

Published by Knight Falls Media 2021

Copyright © 2020 by Penny Knight
ISBN - 978-0-6450308-2-2 (ebook)
ISBN - 978-0-6450308-3-9 (paperback)

All rights reserved. No part of this
publication may be reproduced, stored or transmitted in
any form or by any means, electronic, mechanical,
photocopying, recording, scanning, or otherwise without
written permission from the publisher. It is illegal to
copy this book, post it to a website, or distribute it by any
other means without permission.

Acknowledgments

Thank you to these wonderful professionals.

Book Cover – Knight Falls Media
Editing and Proofreading - Proofreadingbythepage
Symbol Design - https://www.fiverr.com/santagrinina

THE IMMORTALIES SERIES
A NOVELLA

Dedication
Thankyou, Renee and Julie.
Without your support this wouldn't have been possible
And to my own chosen one,
my daughter.

1

The Ride Along

"Is that what you're going to wear?" Topher asks, handing me a cup of freshly brewed coffee when I enter the kitchen.

I take it and raise an eyebrow at him. "What's wrong with what I'm wearing?" I blow the rim to cool the black liquid before it touches my lip.

"Nothing, I guess," he shrugs. "If you weren't planning on getting laid." He closes the laptop and sits taller, leaning on the kitchen counter. "Really Elita, jeans and a t-shirt. Hardly date material."

I laugh.

"I'm not going on a date."

"You're hoping she's gonna have sex with you, right? That's a date."

"Wrong. I'm paying her to have sex with me." I reach over the counter and pinch off a slice of his toast. "She can shove it if she doesn't like my clothes." I give him a wide smile, then take a big bite.

"Mm." With my mouth still full, I ask, "Did you make this bread?"

He grins. "You likey?"

I nod. Topher loves to cook and bake, it makes him happy and it makes me happy to eat the fruits of his labour.

"You know what?" Topher crosses his arms. "You shouldn't be going alone."

Here we go. He has already told me his concerns, but I have taken every precaution I can. This is my first solo investigation, so completing the objective is my number one priority. Even if I am not one hundred percent on board with Tony's plan.

"I'll be fine. I'm meeting her at a café on Rundle street, with plenty of people around." Saturdays are always busy on Rundle street with cafes and bars lining the entire strip. I will be safe there, in public, with lots of traffic.

"It's crazy she agreed to meet a stranger about this over lunch. Is that normal?" He says what I am already thinking.

I shrug. "No idea, I've never hired a sex worker before." It's also not something I want to do again. With the voice recorder in my bag and the money filled envelope ready to go, I'm set to tackle this case, good or bad. "We have to get her admitting she is a prostitute or pushing or using drugs. That's what her ex says in the report anyway for the custody hearing."

I was quite happy with my backstory; she seemed to buy it when I told her my husband wanted to add another person into the bedroom. She bought it when I said I was nervous someone else would interfere in our relationship. It was her to suggest we meet beforehand. So I would be more comfortable.

I look down at the ten-dollar wedding ring I picked up at the discount store which, had it been the real deal, would have hit my imaginary husband's pocket hard. With everything set, I'm ready to go. This needs to go well; I need to prove to Tony I can handle myself.

"I want to come with you," Topher announces.

"Nope." I shake my head as I place the now empty cup on the counter. "Your assignment's due and it's worth half your grade."

"I don't want you to go by yourself. What if her pimp rocks up?"

"How do you know she has a pimp?"

He shrugs. "Don't all of them have pimps? Surely some form of protection?"

"Even if her pimp is there, you've just turned eighteen. Not to sound like a bitch, but if a big gust of wind comes, pretty sure you'd blow away."

I love Topher and his protectiveness over me, but I

would be more worried about him if it involved him.

He throws his other piece of toast at me. It falls on the counter face up.

"You shouldn't throw food. There are starving people out there." I pick it up and eat the rest of his breakfast.

"You are a bitch, but how am I supposed to get any work done when all I'm going to think about is you getting drugged and then trafficked overseas?"

What? My mouth drops open. "Are you serious?" That's a stretch, even for Topher's imagination.

"Very! I was chatting with cygog59 and he said there's a huge market for it on the dark web."

"Ahh, ok." I nod when I realise he is referring to one of his computer buddies. "Whatever. You know he's a big conspiracy theorist. Even if that is true, which sadly it is, I'll park on the main street and make sure I'm not followed when I leave, ok?"

His worried eyes look back at me. I can't take it when he gives me those eyes. 'Don't," I snap at him, but that only makes him pout more.

"I'll stay in the car," he promises as he drops his bottom lip.

I screw up my face. Is he really going to stoop this low?

"Listen, if I try to write my assignment now, I will probably stuff it up, then I'd have to pull an all-nighter this weekend to fix it." He pulls the laptop closer to him. With one hand he rubs the back of his neck and winces in pain. "My neck is already getting stiff."

"Oh, for goodness' sake, get in the bloody car," I concede, like he knew I would.

What a surprise, his pain disappears. He seizes the piece of toast right from my hand as he runs to the front door.

"Don't even think about eating in my new car," I yell out after him.

~

It's a good thing we left early because we had to circle the block ten times before someone pulled out of a parking space across from the café. I glance back at the car and spot Topher with his camera. He insisted he wanted to record the interaction for my safety. I agreed, only because it worried me that the audio evidence might not be enough in the family courts. The problem is, Topher is too excited about joining me on my assignment. He keeps bugging me to ask Tony for a job.

I love my job, I'm good at it, and I felt like it's what I was meant to do. School was never for me. I was such an introvert; I had trouble making friends and never wanted to be there. Maybe it was because my mother ran out on me when I was a child, that I had a general disdain and mistrust of people most of my life. Being a private investigator is a perfect fit. My job specifically requires me to not be seen or discovered. It's my perfect place to hide.

But Topher is so incredibly smart. He is a whiz with computers. It blew me away when he first came to live with me at fourteen. He could take apart and upgrade my hunky old computer, turning it into a usable device in no time, and with little money. Which there wasn't much of. He has too much talent to not pursue a career in technology or medicine or whatever he sets his heart on. He deserves better than a job that before today was me, sitting in a car watching a door for ten hours a day. I have been on stakeouts only until I finished my course and got my licence. Today is my first real undercover case. I've got three months before Topher graduates. That is plenty of time to convince him that university is the right choice for him.

"Sarah?" A scratchy voice from behind me pulls me out of my musings. I turn and look up at the woman who calls herself Ruby, recognising her from her online profile. Bright red hair pulled in a tight ponytail. She wears her short, and I mean really short, leopard print skirt well. It almost takes my eye away from her black V-neck blouse that dips down to her navel. Here we go.

"Yes, I'm Sarah." I smile thinking she isn't the only one with a fake name today. "You must be Ruby?" I ask, letting some nervous energy seep into my voice.

"The one and only." She returns my smile and pulls out the chair opposite. I chose the table furthest away from the other patrons. It just so happens it's also close to the road and I'm hoping Topher has a clear shot of us from where he's hunkered down in the back seat of my new car.

"Thank you for meeting me." My voice is quiet, awkward. I'm biding my time before I reel her in. I've got a running loop of Tony barking out instructions in my head. But he isn't here. It's just me, and I have to pull this off if I want him to give me the big jobs.

"No problem." She looks down at the empty table and says, "No drinks?"

She just sat down. Did she expect me to read her mind and have her favourite drink waiting for her? I bite down my thoughts hampering my initial response. "Would you like a drink?" I ask and smile sweetly.

"Yeah, sounds good." She picks up the drinks menu and I watch as she studies the cocktail list. Tony better give me back the money I'm spending on her.

She catches a server's eye and beckons her over. The entitlement oozes from her pores.

"How are you, ladies?" The bubbly server asks as she pulls out her notepad. "What can I get for you?"

"Mmm..." Ruby mulls over the menu. It gives me time to appreciate her makeup, a little heavy-handed but perfect, aside from the red rim around her nose. If I were to guess, it's from the white powder she allegedly sells. "I think I'll try a Eucalyptus Martini."

A what?

I snatch up the other menu from the table. Right there, listed under the cocktails, a twenty-dollar Eucalyptus Martini. Bile rises as I envision drinking what Franziska makes me diffuse when I'm sick. Maybe the red nose isn't because of the drugs after all. Maybe she just has a cold.

I gently place down the menu. "I will just have sparkling water."

She writes our order, then disappears back into the restaurant.

"So, tell me about your husband." Ruby takes her sunglasses off her head and starts putting them in her case as she waits for me to respond.

My husband. Ok. "Uh, he is a very busy man. He works extremely hard."

She looks me up and down. My makeup consists of just foundation, a little eyeliner, and mascara. My long brown hair hangs in loose waves down my back, and as her judgy eyes roam over me, I'm re-thinking what Topher said about changing. That is until her eyes land on my fake diamond ring and she sits up straighter and leans more into the table. I can see the dollar signs spin in her eyes. Poor Ruby, she has no idea.

I wonder where her three-year-old daughter is while she is meeting me. Hopefully, in day-care instead of the foyer of her brothel, like the statement the ex-husband has given.

"So, you want to give him a little present, huh?" She

winks. "Good on you for knowing how you keep your man happy and not being a prude."

To each their own, I guess.

I nod, not having anything more to add. "He takes care of me, so why not? Not gonna lie, I am a little nervous though."

"No need to be nervous. Is this an ongoing thing or just a one-off fuck fest?"

Don't react, don't react, don't react, I chant in my head. I stare at the menu and will my face not to move. Thank God I didn't let Topher sit at the table next to me like he begged.

"I'm not sure." I say when I make eye contact with her again. My blood starts to boil as she sits there all smug and smiles down at me. She relishes at watching me squirm. She thinks she makes me feel insecure when put on the spot. She thrives on it. Of the power she thinks she wields. I can see the glint in her eyes. Not only is she a horrible mother, if what her ex-husband says is true, but she is a horrible person, as well. Trust me, I know all about horrible mothers. And it is with that loathsome thought that any shred of guilt I felt, before coming here, vanishes. It. Is. On.

The server comes back with our drinks and we both take a large gulp. Ruby beats me though, as she downs all of hers in one go. She's dreaming if she thinks I'm going to buy her another one.

"I'm nervous. I have never done anything like this before." It is time to force my mind back on track. I play up the image she has of me. The shy, timid wife. I want her to assume I'm vulnerable and in need of pharmaceutical help, but she needs to feel as though she can coax me into a deal. "Like I said over messages, I thought I would look into this instead of trying online to find someone."

"Don't go online. Trust me. Once a man gets inside another woman, it gets complicated unless it's paid for. This way, feelings won't get involved and we all can have a little fun."

With that remark, I'm one hundred percent convinced I could not do this in real life. The thought of my husband inside another woman makes me mad, and even though my husband is imaginary, I already want to chop off his wiener.

She's not afraid at all to talk. The more she does, the more information I'm getting. It's good, but still isn't quite a true confession.

I look around, feeling a little uncomfortable. No one seems to pay attention to us. I fiddle with my hair as she giggles to herself.

I am well past pissed off now. Granted, it doesn't take much, but where is her professionalism? Who laughs at a potential customer? Fake or not.

"Oh honey, lighten up." She does a shimmy in her seat. "Maybe this is just what your marriage needs. No offence, but you seem a little uptight. It's probably why he wants to spice it up."

I want to throw this drink in her face. Instead, I smile. "You're right," I say with a sigh. "This is just not how I was raised." I give her a small, sad, pathetic smile. "I'm just scared I will freeze up when we are... you know." My eyes drop, I act shy.

"You'll be fine. I'm the best at what I do. Plus," she leans forward, "I might have something that can help you with that."

Hook, line and sinker.

"Really?" I lean forward. "Like homework?"

She laughs out loud.

Keep laughing at me sweetheart, you wait for the review I am going to leave you. What am I talking about, where am I meant to review her services?

"Oh my god." She takes a deep breath. "Aren't you precious? No, I don't mean homework, although that might not be a bad idea for you. I mean something to take the edge off."

I bite my lip to portray this conversation makes me a little nervous but intrigued. Even though I have been the one feeding her this crap and leading her right where I want her.

"Did you bring the money?" she asks.

I nod. "Yes, you said $500 right? Half now and half after?" If you ask me, that is steep.

"Look, I can get you something to help you with that money and you fix me up on the night for my services."

I lean forward and whisper, "You mean like drugs?"

This makes her look around and hiss, "Shh." Her demeanour changes. "Keep it quiet, would you?"

"Sorry," I add quickly.

"Yes, ok. Did you still want this for next Saturday night?"

I nod.

"So, are we all good? Should I book you in?" she pushes.

"Yes. For both, I think." I lean forward again. "For the sex and the drugs," I say just above a whisper. This I need on tape.

Her eyes are wide.

I pretend to be nervous again.

"Fine, deal," she says. She sits back and then extends her open hand out to me.

Ok, she wants that money now I take it. Leaning to the side, I pick up my backpack. Whilst I look for the envelope Tony gave me with the money, I double-check that my recorder is working. The red flashing light blinks back at me and confirms it.

I pull out the envelope and hand it over to her.

With a whopping smile, she takes it out of my hand.

As soon as it hits her grip, all hell breaks loose.

"Don't move," a loud, deep male's voice booms over

the scraping of chairs. Out of nowhere, two large men appear, flashing badges as they run towards the table.

Ruby bolts, the chair flies to the floor as she tries to flee down the footpath. A rough hand pulls me up and out of my chair.

"What the fuck?" I yell as I feel cold metal slap over my wrist.

"Don't move, you're under arrest for solicitation."

My mouth drops open. "This is a mistake." I try to plea, but it just makes the cuffs cinch my wrists when I resist. I watch Ruby run through traffic, cars having to stop as a cop tackles her to the ground right in front of my car.

Holy shit.

Planted in the car window, I see Topher's horrified face and his damn camera.

I am going to kill Tony for this.

2

The Assignment

The forming crowd watches Ruby swear and kick violently. She gets pulled from the ground and thrown into the back of a waiting police panel wagon.

I am being led to another police car not making a sound. Unlike Ruby, I try very hard to melt into the pavement to disappear from this embarrassment.

Topher pops his head out of the car window, mouth open, about to call out to me. I don't trust he won't say something that could hurt the case or get Tony in trouble, so I cut him off before he speaks.

"Call Tony and get him to meet me at..." I pause. Where are they taking me? I strain my neck to turn and see who is manhandling me. That's when I see green eyes peering down at me. "Where are we going?" I ask the cop.

"Adelaide Station," his deep voice answers.

We are getting further away from my car, so I crane my neck to see him. "Adelaide Police Station. Get Tony there," I yell to Topher.

His panicked nods show me he understood what I said, but he does something that I did not expect.

He jumps into the driver's seat. My mouth drops open. I said call, not get in my ten thousand dollar Supra I saved and scrimped for. No one has driven my baby, especially Topher, who is only on his permits.

I'm going to rip him a new one for that.

"Watch your head." This touch is less forceful as the cop guides my head into the waiting police car.

"Wait, this is a mistake," I try again.

"Yeah, yeah, I am sure it is," his snooty reply has my mouth hanging open as my butt hits the cold vinyl seats.

"Yeah, yeah, and I'm sure you're not a complete ass, either," I mumble.

The sound of the seatbelt stops, but I refuse to look at the cop. I know he heard me and I am so pissed I don't care at all.

The slow grind of the belt continues, and his large body now is in my space. I lean into the backseat, trying to put as much distance between us as I can. With my hands behind my back, it causes my chest to push out, making it even more awkward.

I pretend not to notice and avoid further humiliation.

My eyes stay fixed on the street sign out of the window. He clicks my belt in, and like a child I am safely tucked away.

"Word of advice, sweetheart," he says as I roll my eyes. "Why don't you wait for your husband before you let that mouth of yours get you in trouble?"

I scoff and shake my head. My stupid fake husband, he can fuck himself after this.

"Right, ok. I shall wait for my master. I am but a measly useless woman. Unable to think and speak for herself." This time I look at him. Not his face, but his hands. I notice his lack of a ring on his finger. "Oh what a surprise, you're not married."

He synchs the belt tighter. Crap. Now I can't move an inch. His face is eye level to mine and close. Close enough to see the amber specks in his green eyes.

"For such an independent woman, you really went above and beyond to obey your weak husband's demands," the cop says.

I snap my head forward and narrow my eyes at his smiling, damn it, handsome face.

"My husband is not weak." I need to stop. I don't even have a husband.

"He got you out here paying for a hooker, yeah?" His cocky eyebrow raises.

If he thinks I was born yesterday and about to give my confession in the back seat of this smelly police car, he can think again.

I slam my mouth shut, lift my chin and look out through the window. I would flip him the bird, but my hands are literally tied behind my back.

He chuckles.

I grind my teeth.

"Get comfy," he says as he stands. "Courts aren't open till Monday. You got an entire weekend to think about if he's worth it."

My mouth drops open as the door slams in my face.

~

The grey dull interview room is a few degrees cooler than it needs to be. I rub the goose bumps forming on my shoulder. At least they released me from the cuffs for processing.

It has been hours since they arrested me; they read me my rights, fingerprinted me, and took what photos they needed and plopped me in this dinky room.

I should be grateful I'm not sitting in a cell, but I have an uneasy feeling that is coming next.

The door creaks open and the big-muscled cop that arrested me strides into the room. His uniform straining to fit over his large biceps, the long sleeve shirt not covering all of what looks to be a sleeve tattoo starting at his wrist and peeking out from his collar.

His eyes look down at a file, I assume my file. He drags

the metal chair on the concrete floor.

"Let's get straight to it," he says, still shuffling through the file. Really? What could be in there? I have never been in trouble before.

I lean my head on my hand as I wait for him to continue.

"Let's start with your name?" He looks up.

"You don't have it in that huge file there?" I know I should be nice, he is only doing his job, but I was only doing mine, too. Now, I'm at a loss. If I tell him the truth, would it get Tony in trouble? Would I get fired?

I really hope he is out there trying to fix this.

"It is, but I'd like you to confirm it." He doesn't smile anymore.

I sigh, "Elita Machiavelli."

"Not Sarah?" he asks.

I close my mouth. Is lying to a prostitute a crime? Possibly fraud? It's safest to keep my mouth shut on that one.

I don't answer.

My eyes dart around, trying to avoid his waiting ones on me.

"Ok, where did you find Ruby? Was she referred to you? Did your husband suggest her?"

I don't want to rat on Tony or dig myself into any holes. My best bet is to keep my mouth shut, as much as I can. With that, I keep my eyes down on the table.

"Uh, so now you're gonna listen to me?" He leans

back in his chair.

"I wouldn't go that far," I mumble under my breath.

"Right." He leans forward. "Elita, you know they have arrested you for soliciting and procuring prostitution?"

I nod. "What's the penalty for that?" Apart from it being on my record for life. There goes any other job prospects with that splashed all across my background records.

His lack of response has me looking up.

I raise my brows, waiting. "Maximum penalty of $750," he says.

I laugh. I don't even mean to. "$750? That's it. No jail or anything?" I relax into my chair. Thank god, I mean I can't afford $750 now, especially since I just gave my savings as a deposit on a rented warehouse apartment in Port Adelaide that Topher and I just moved into, but no jail sounds great to me.

"Not for that, but we haven't gotten to your drug charge. That comes with a max penalty of ten thousand and a two-year imprisonment." His eyes lock on to mine.

I close mine and take a deep breath in. This is ridiculous.

"Elita," he says my name again, this time dropping the sharp edge of his tone. It has me looking up. "I'm sure this will get settled quick in court. I just need to know how you got into contact with her and then run through your statement of events."

"So, you say that I could look at two years and in the

next breath you say it's fine and will be settled in court quick? That makes no sense." I rub my forehead.

"By the size of the ring, I'm sure your lawyers can afford to wrap this up quick." His disdain is eminent in his voice.

"Oh, my god." I rip the ring off my finger. "This ring's like ten fucking dollars." I throw it on the table.

He frowns and a blooming redness creeps up from his neck. "He got you a fucking fake ring?"

"No, Mr. Judgy." I shake my head. "There is no husband. No money, no lawyer, nothing. But I am done answering your questions. I plead the fifth." I don't know what that really means, I have seen it in movies so many times it sounds like something I should say right about now."

It's quiet as he studies me.

I drop my head on the table in my arms and groan.

"There are no constitutional rights of silence in Australia, I think you mean to say, 'No comment'. Is that right Miss," he elaborates the Miss, "Machiavelli?"

With one eye, I look to him and nod.

He closes the folder.

"I will get someone to escort you to the holding cell, you can make a phone before then and if you decide you want to help with the investigation, tell the handling officer to contact Constable Malloy."

With that, he stands. I stay where I am and resign

myself to not getting out of here until Monday, lucky I didn't have any other plans this weekend other than me celebrating my first case.

Congratulations Elita, a job well done.

~

"The prosecution has conversed with the defence. Considering the circumstances, we propose the charges be dropped, Your Honour."

Five minutes.

That is how long I have been sitting in the defendant's hot seat. Five minutes for the Prosecutor to advise the judge to drop the charges.

Five measly minutes.

I was in the cold concrete, wee infested cell for one whole night for five pathetic minutes. The lawyer had prepared me for this briefly when I met them. The lawyer that hired us for the initial reason I'm here.

With the bang of the gavel, I'm a free woman again. Topher jumps up, but Tony holds him back from jumping over the bannister in the courtroom to give me a hug.

I smile at him as I make my way, ushered by the court martial to the back of the room where I am led out to a holding area waiting on the paperwork.

Finally, this nightmare is over. I need a shower, a change of clothes, and some nutritional food that is not off a deep-fried menu. But most of all, I want my bed and a good night's sleep.

The glass motorised doors open from the courthouse to a waiting Topher and Tony. I don't make it three feet out of the door before I am wrapped in a bear hug.

"I was so worried, are you ok?" Topher squeezes.

"I'm fine." I pull back. "But why are you not at school?"

"Are you serious? As if I was going to miss this," he says, his eyes wide.

Tony slaps me on the right shoulder. "What the hell happened? How the fuck did you get yourself arrested?"

"Me?" I screech. "How the hell is this my fault? I told you it was a dumb idea to begin with."

"What are you talking about? She got locked up. Case closed, we won. Good job, Elita."

"Good. Job?" I throw my hands up. "I spent a night in jail because of you."

"It was a holding cell, not jail, relax." He grabs his ringing phone from his pocket and holds up a finger to me as he goes to answer the call.

"Uh, no way. We aren't finished with this." I call after him as he walks away. But I freeze as I see a tall, blond-haired, muscled man leaning on the light pole. A familiar tattooed officer.

Constable Malloy.

I frown, it can't be a coincidence.

It's not. He holds something up to me I can't make out this far away.

"Wait here," I say to Topher. "I will be back in a sec."

He turns to see what I am looking at. "Where are you - Oh wait, is that the cop from the video?"

I swing my head back as I walk. "What video?"

"E, oh my god you should see the video. It's epic. I think it might even go viral."

"What!" I turn to him. "You better be joking."

He shuts his mouth and looks up to the sky as his foot circles around.

"Wait till we get home." I point at him.

Then I storm towards the cop that only a day ago had me in cuffs, and not in the good way, either.

"You could have just said you had your PI licence," he says as I stop in front of him.

I shrug. "I didn't want to get my boss in trouble."

"Your boss shouldn't have sent you alone on an assignment like that." He leaves no room for argument and I am too tired anyway.

I sigh.

He opens his hand and holds out the object he was trying to show me.

My ten dollar ring.

I smile.

So does he.

"Thought you might want to keep this for a reminder," he says as he hands me back my ring.

I take it and scoff, "Of me getting arrested? Right."

He chuckles, "Nah, because it was when we first met."

This time I laugh but feel my cheeks warming up. "Is that right?" I shake my head.

"I think it's a great story to tell our kids."

"That I was arrested hiring a prostitute? Uh no, that is not appropriate to tell our kids." Then I realise what I said. "I mean kids in general. Not our kids. Because we won't be having kids."

"Why? You don't want to have a family? It's not a problem if so, but we probably need to iron out the nuts and bolts before we get to that." His lopsided grin making the warmth now flow from my cheeks to other places.

"Judgy and cocky, huh?" I smile as his laughter sounds deep and soulful in the air.

He stops laughing, and his green eyes lay on mine. "Have dinner with me?"

I look down. "I don't think so."

"Why not?"

"Because." This time it's my foot that is doing small circles on the footpath.

"Because why?" he questions again.

"Jesus, what are you, a cop?"

We both laugh.

"Seriously, I'm just concentrating on work at the moment. I'm not dating."

He bites down on his lip as I realise how dumb that sounds since my work has gotten me locked up over the weekend.

"A drink?" he insists.

"YES!" I hear Topher yell from behind me.

I swing my head around to meet him. "Shut it, you."

I turn back to see the cop's wide smile looking at me.

"I don't even know your name?"

"Brian," he says without hesitation.

"Fine, one drink. No dating and no talk of children," I lay out my terms.

"Anything you want, darlin'." He smiles his lop-sided grin again.

Oh boy, this guy is no doubt trouble.

3

The Test

SIX MONTHS LATER

His gentle, warm touch on my shoulder puts a smile on my face. It's not the ringing of the alarm that has woken me in a good mood. It's the after glow of another amazing night.

I open one eye. "Morning," I say.

Brian hovers over me as he generously turns off the alarm. His lips also find their way to mine. "Morning, beautiful," he says after a sweet morning kiss.

He pulls me into him with one strong arm and I certainly don't resist. I'm not only getting used to waking like this, but I am starting to love it.

I swallow the lump from that heady thought.

It might be time for him to stay at his house for a bit. We have been spending a lot of time together. Mostly naked, but still his here most nights at the dinner table with us. I only meant this to be casual.

"Today's the big day," he reminds me.

"I know, I'm nervous for him." I sucked on my high school exams, just passing. Topher will be more than fine. He's so much smarter than I am. Not street smart, but he understands things that hurt my head even thinking of. I know he is going to knock it out of the park.

Brian opens his fingers wider under my back. His hand roams until he grips around my waist, pulling me on top of him as he lays back on the bed.

I like this, as well.

I show him by lowering my mouth and kissing his. Like the first night he took me dancing and got me drunk. As soon as my lips touch his, the kiss deepens from innocent to wanting more. So much more.

I feel he wants it, too, and I position myself and move my hips, his deep moan letting me know there is no more room for conversation. He is already rock hard, and it rubs all the right places.

Brian pulls me into his chest and holds the back of my neck, as he kisses me deeper and deeper. There is no barrier between us, the nuts and bolts like he calls it have been fastened. We don't need protection; we have done our due diligence.

With one hand I stroke him, not breaking apart our fevered kiss. I guide him inside me, slowly. Taking control, inching him, savouring the fullness.

Over the last six months, it's been the mornings Brian doesn't insist on being in control. He seems to enjoy letting me have my morning fun. He lays back and lets me give us both what we need, with me in charge.

His kisses stop as he finds my neck, struggling for control as he hits the limit buried inside me.

I don't give him relief; I move straight away. Up and down rhythmically to his heavy breathing.

"Fuck." His hand snakes back around into my hair, turning me to face him again, crushing his lips on mine as I go faster and faster.

It builds for me like it does for him. Our bodies connected, close to the edge where we both desperately want to be.

His hands unable to stay away, he caresses my body as he makes his way down to my waist, over to my hips.

I know what he is doing. He wants the control back. No way.

I sit up, grabbing his hands and planting them above his head.

"Fuck." He thrusts into me.

I don't stop, I'm so close. A moan escapes, this time from me as pleasure builds within.

Brian's body picking up on my pleasure brings him to his release.

"Elita, fuck. I love you." He thrusts and rides out his

orgasm, eyes closed and completely unaware I have frozen.

Holy shit, the pleasure rips through me as his last thrust tips me over the edge, overloading my senses and my brain processing what was just said.

Our breathing returns to normal, his hand caresses my body, but it is not until his eyes open and he meets my gaze that I realise my throat is closing up. Like an anaconda is constricting around my body, squeezing the air out of me.

"Elita." His deep voice has that tone. The tone he has every now and again, one that I have avoided hearing.

The tone of one about to say those three words.

The three words he just said.

The three words I did not want to here.

A loud shatter breaks both of our thoughts, followed by a deafening scream. I fly off the bed and throw my dressing gown over my naked body.

Whatever it is, I have never been so grateful for the sound of breaking glass.

"Elita, wait," Brian calls out. I look back as I see him hopping on one leg, trying to put pants on quickly.

"Later, ok? I have to see what happened."

I don't wait. I run. I bolt. I think I even flew out the room. That's how fast I wanted out of the conversation we were about to have.

~

"Keep your arm up." I look back at the blood-soaked towel wrapped around Topher's forearm. He has it drooped over his lap. Blood has almost hit the seats.

"It hurts." He winces but listens, propping his elbow up on the door rest.

"I bet it does. You cut yourself pretty good there," Brian says as he overtakes another car. The only other conversation we've had since the whole I love you debacle, was him insisting on coming and driving Topher to the hospital.

"What am I going to do? My exam is at twelve today." Topher lunges forward, holding the car seat with his good hand.

"Look, I'm sure it will be ok. I'm sure there is another time you can take it." I try to reassure him.

"What?" He throws both hands up, forgetting about the cut. "Ow, mother fu-" he bites down hard on his lip and tenses, riding out the wave of pain.

The cut definitely needs stitches. It's deep, but it all depends on him and the hospital. There is a possibility that he could make it on time, but even a hard ass like me won't make him go.

"That is bullshit." Topher sits back in his chair.

"I'm with you there," Brian mumbles, looking over his shoulder indicating to overtake again.

How fast is he going?

I shake my head. He isn't talking about Topher missing

his exam, but he just keeps on driving. He hasn't forgotten about this morning, and it looks like this time he might not drop it.

With a heavy sigh, I sink back into the seat. This is not the day I had envisioned.

"Get out of town," Topher calls out. "Are you two having your first fight?" He sounds way too excited about that, and I whip my head around.

"No," I say.

"Yes," Brian says.

Great, now this is really going to set Topher off. At least it will take his mind off his injury for a bit. Problem is, this is not at all what I want to talk about. Now, ever, and especially not in front of Topher.

"What the hell could have happened from last night till now? I had to listen to Vengaboys on repeat for hours trying to drown the two of you out, just to get to sleep."

"First, Vengaboys? That's what you listen to as your drifting off to sleep?" I ask because really, who does that?

"As if you wouldn't want to dream of a mobile disco bus every night?" He looks at me like I'm the one that said the most outrageous thing. "And don't try that with me." He turns his attention to Brian. "Fun Fact. Sunshine here is Queen of the diversion tactic."

Traitor.

It's lucky Brian is driving, I'd hardly slow down before I'd kick his ass out on the doorstep of Emergency.

"You don't have to worry about me," Brian says. "I picked that one up a long time ago. Problem is, eventually there is nowhere else to look."

"You know what?" I cross my arms. "I am right here Confucius, you don't need to speak in fancy riddles."

Topher barks out a laugh.

This gets Brian's attention off the road and his gaze on me. "Good. Actually, that's fucking great." The car comes to a stop in traffic behind a school bus. "I tell you I love you and you bolt? Whats up with that?"

Oops. I got led straight into that.

It's oddly quiet in the back. Just like in the front seat where I am. I don't know what to say because I don't know the answer to his question myself.

I check in on Topher. As suspected, his mouth is open season for any wayward fly. He sits there stunned.

I turn my attention to Brian. His sunglasses hide his eyes but I don't need to see them to know he isn't angry, I hear the hurt in his voice. Even if he tried to hide it.

We sit, eyes locked. Guilt and fear brewing inside me like a steaming hot tea.

"I don't know what to say." It's the truest thing I can tell him.

He nods.

He looks forward and without reacting to the beeping coming from behind us, he continues driving.

No one talks as we turn into the carpark of the Queen

Elizabeth Hospital.

    I know what he wants me to say.

    I know what I want to say.

    I just don't think that I can.

~

    Hospitals bring out the quiet in people. It does for me. The hours we spent waiting were done with Brian making calls and Topher trying to talk to me about what happened in the car.

    This meant I was actively working, doing anything I could to detract from the questions.

    I am the queen of distraction after all.

    Now, we sit after the doctor has finished with the last stitch, waiting for the script so we can go home.

    By the smile on Topher's face and the starry eyes I saw from him as he watched the good-looking doctor walk away, he doesn't feel pain anymore. Thanks to the local anaesthetic and pain killers he is on cloud nine.

    "You all good?" I ask, just to make sure.

    "Yeah, I can't feel it much now," Topher says. "What time is it?"

    "Quarter to twelve," Brian says, looking at his watch.

    Only fifteen minutes until his test.

    Topher's smile fades. "Do you think we can make it?"

    "Huh?" Surely he doesn't want to go. "I don't know. I

don't think so. Plus, you're all pharmed up now."

"I'm fine, Elita. I have studied my ass off, even though you know how I feel about it. I want to work with you." I sigh, he hasn't stopped since Brian arrested me. He is hellbent on joining the PI business after school finishes. "It still doesn't mean that I don't hear what you say all the time. I want to do this test and I want to smash it. I want my options open, and after all you have done for me. I can't just give up now. I just don't know if I will make it in time."

I jump up. He wants to smash the test. Then he is going to smash the test. "Are you serious, have you seen this guy drive?" I point to Brian, then turn to him with a smile that comes from my soul. A place where Topher made me feel so proud of how far he has come. How far we have both come. "Do you think you can get us there in time?"

"With enough time to sharpen your pencils," Brian says to Topher, then returns my smile.

And there it is. Even though he is angry with me, and I have probably hurt him with my silence, he still will go out of his way for me. For us. My heart swells.

I clap. "Let's go." I scoop up my bag.

Topher jumps off the bed. "Wait, my script."

"We don't have time." My hand has the door waiting open for him as Brian already makes his way down the hall.

"Shit, this is gonna suck in four hours," he says, but he falls in line as we hustle out of the emergency department.

We aren't parked far, and Brian has the car running before Topher has even opened the door.

And like he does every day in his life, Brian drives like he is playing a fast track game of chess. He knows the timing of the lights, the flow of the traffic. His trained skills have us weaving through traffic. No matter how many lessons he teaches me about attack and defensive driving techniques, no way will I be as confident as him. We make it there in time, and if Topher really wanted to, enough time to sharpen his pencils.

Crap. He doesn't have pencils.

Hopefully, he can borrow off someone else. "Good luck," I call out to him as he disappears behind the front doors of his school.

Finally, a huge feeling of relief.

And now, it's just us.

I turn to Brian, who is leaned up against his truck.

A deep inhale gives me the grounding I need and the confidence to walk in front of him.

He watches and waits, but doesn't leave me hanging. He hooks his finger into my belt loop and pulls me in closer.

But he still does not speak first.

"I don't know how to do this." My voice doesn't even sound like my own. Soft and vulnerable, I can even hear the fear in it.

"Neither do I," he says. "I know I want to, though.

And I know you love me Elita, I see it in all the small things you do for me. The things you think you can get away with showing me. I see it."

My eyes well and I try to look away, but he stops me with his index finger under my chin. "Can you let me love you and all that goes with it?" he asks.

I shake my head. His brows crease. "I'm really not sure, Brian. You say you want to take care of me and for me to let you, but that is not something I can do."

"Why?" he asks.

"Because I have always needed to just take care of myself. Yeah I know, Franziska took me in and I am so grateful and love her but she was kind of weird and even then it was always just me."

It was always me that had to look out for myself, dangers, predators. Growing up with the mother I had, I learned a specific set of survival tools at a very young age. Sex is just sex. That I can do. Very well. But letting someone in scares me to my core.

"I don't know if I can keep doing this, without having it all with you." Brian's voice breaks.

Even though a part of me knew we would get to this point, I never realised how the thought of not having him in my life would be so debilitating. There is a sinking feeling in the pit of my stomach that's making the bile rise just at the thought of it. Loss. A loss that I am choosing to do to myself.

I shake my head, eyes now clearly teared. "Well," I clear the lump in my throat. I guess I need to put on my big girl pants, and see that the man in front of me loves me, damage and all. I take a deep, long inhale, and like an out-of-body experience, I say the words that have had me shook since I felt them.

"I love you, Brian."

~

"Change and food." I clap and bounce in my seat. The car stops on the street of our two-story warehouse apartment. We pile out. I'm in desperate need of a shower to freshen up before dinner. Brian booked at our favourite restaurant to celebrate Topher smashing his exam.

According to him, he did just that.

"Best day ever!" Topher booms.

I smile. Overall, I might just have to agree. "Topher, get ready because I'm gonna get you drunk." He cheers at my announcement.

"And I don't even need a fake ID anymore." He does a shimmy.

Brian coughs. Both Topher and I laugh.

"Who is that?" Brian nods, looking forward.

Following his gaze, I squint to see a man and woman at the door of our apartment. Clean, well dressed, they turn and their eyes light up.

"No idea. But they seem to know us," I say. Maybe not us, but one of us. They are looking at....

"Mum?" Topher looks from the woman to the man. "Dad?" He answers our question.

And just in a blink of an eye, the tilt of my world has gone off its axis.

4

The Dinner

WEDNESDAY

My fingers slip off the zipper for the third time, and my arms are getting sore trying to zip the back of my dress. Clenching my fist tight, I close my eyes and will my patience and anger to subside so I can do the basic of tasks, like getting dressed.

"Seriously, babe. Let me do it." Brian comes up behind me.

"Fine." I slump and look in the full-length mirror. I've had a quick shower; Topher and his parents are waiting downstairs, and I'm mad out of my mind. I don't know why, but they are coming with us to dinner.

"You're shaking." Brian's fingers caress my shoulder.

"Because I'm furious." I use my free hands now to massage my temples and forehead, trying to relieve the tension.

"I can see." He slowly zips the rest of my dress. "Why?"

I swing around to face him. "Why?" I huff. "First, why are they coming for dinner?"

"You mean Topher's parents?"

"Uh, yeah, who else would I be talking about?" I scrunch up my face.

He lets a small chuckle out. "I know I don't know the backstory here. But, it's not unusual for parents to want to see their son on their graduation."

"That's a stretch calling them parents." I roll my eyes. "Who leaves their kid with an alcoholic uncle to take off on a pilgrimage for eight years? What? Did they get fucking lost?" Brian's mouth opens to talk, but I hold my finger up. "Plus, it isn't his graduation. He just took his exams. How dumb are they?"

"Okay, okay." He fights his smile, which is wise because I'm not smiling at all. "That was me that said that, not them. So let's put the pitchfork down a second." I raise my brows. "Wait, here me out."

"Ok." I cross my arms. "Let's hear it"

He smiles this time. "Topher invited them to join us, he looked a bit freaked, so he will probably need your support through this dinner, especially if he hasn't seen them in all that time."

"Well, why can't I support him by helping to throw

their asses to the curb?" He drops his head, lost for words but chuckling. "Also, he didn't really have a choice. Did you see them fishing for the invite?"

He looks up, smiling, before it fades when he sees how serious I am. "What do you need me to do?"

I sigh and reply, "I don't know." What I want to do and what I should do are two very different things. One, I'd probably end up locked up again, the other is me grinning and bearing a dinner with two people that make me utterly sick. I sigh, "Just kick me under the table if I am being too much of a bitch."

"I won't kick you, but I will find a way." He shrugs. "Although, I do kind of love the bitch side, too, not gonna lie."

This makes me smile. "What a surprise." We all know I wasn't Susie Sunshine the day we met.

His arms snake around my waist, pulling me in for a warm, slow kiss, one that I want to explore more, one that makes me want to take this dress off after finally getting it on.

But I can't leave Topher out there on his own any longer. I pull back from Brian but finish with a quick peck.

"Let's see what they have to say for themselves." I smack his bottom. "Let's go."

"Oh shit, here we go." Brian takes my hand in his as we leave the room to have dinner with Topher's absent parents.

~

The small restaurant is tucked away in the middle of Gouger Street in the city. It's our go to for Chinese food, our favourite. Especially before we moved to the westside and out of the city. The best thing about this place is that it's not known for a wine and dine experience. The service is great, fast and efficient, but the constant line at the door pushes the patrons to eat, pay and leave as quick as possible. For this dinner, I couldn't have asked for a better venue.

They have seated us at a small round table at the front. Topher is hiding behind the large one-page menu, even though he already knows it back to front.

In the car ride over, which I refused to let them come with us, Topher was quiet. I asked if he was doing ok and he said it overwhelmed him and it was awkward.

Mary, Topher's mother has perched lips as she surveys the restaurant. No chairs match, they strew tables around in no particular order that makes little sense to anyone other than the wait staff. She smooths down her short blonde blowed out hair. Her eyes catch mine watching her and she plasters on a smile. I want to wipe it off.

"Isn't this place," she pauses, "quaint."

If I were Brian, I would kick myself right about now in advance. Can her disdain be any more obvious?

"Oh, really? What were the Chinese restaurants like

where you were?" My smile reflecting her passive aggressive one. "Where was that again?"

Brian's large hand finds my knee under the table and he strokes his thumb in small circular motions. Too late, buddy. If only he could read my mind, he would have caught up earlier.

"Oh, we have been blessed to have travelled to many wonderful parts of the world," she boasts.

My mouth opens but Brian is catching on quick as he gives me a gentle squeeze. She is lucky because I want to rip her a new one. How dare she talk about how lucky she was to travel the world while she left her son behind?

"It is true, but we are so happy to be back now." Graham, Topher's father adds trying to fix her tone deaf comment. "Tobias, you said you just finished your exams today. How do you think you did?"

Topher's eyes go wide as he looks at me, putting the menu down.

"Tobias?" I frown. Am I missing something here?

"Oh, you don't know my son's proper name?" Mary patronises, and Brian squeezes my knee.

Underneath the table, I remove Brian's hand. I am done. I don't need a filter; I need the pitchfork so I can throw it at her head.

Maybe that is a bit too far.

Brian clears his throat and reaches for his glass of water. No doubt not missing the meaning behind the gesture.

If this bitch wants to play like that, we shall play.

"Guess not. Probably because it sounds dumb." I shrug. Brian spits out his water.

"So sorry," he says as he quickly takes some napkins and cleans up the sprayed water. "Anyway, I like Topher way better, it suits him perfectly." I smile at Topher, a real genuine smile. I don't really have an issue with the name, just the people that gave it to him.

Topher's chest rises and falls as he takes a needed breath. Was he scared I would be angry about it, and why is he being so quiet? This kid can talk underwater. I hate he feels out of sorts so much he can't speak up for himself.

"Excuse me?" Mary asks.

"Oh, what for?" I feign confusion, looking around like I missed something she said or did. Topher puts his hand in front of his mouth, hiding his smile.

She doesn't have time to respond as the server comes to the table. Brian, Topher, and I make quick work of our order whilst Mary asks every question under the sun. Whilst she is distracted busting the server's chops, I turn my attention to Topher. "Are you ok?" I mouth.

He nods and gives a weak smile. I'm going to take it as a no. I don't blame him. I wouldn't know what I would be like if my mother showed up on the doorstep one day.

Well, I wouldn't be breaking bread with her, that's for damn sure.

"So," Graham begins once the server leaves. "Topher,"

he corrects. "How do you think you did on the exams?"

"Ok, I think," Topher replies. Short and sweet. His knee is bouncing around, the nervous energy is lingering in the air.

Along with all the unanswered questions. Why would you leave? Why didn't you take your son? And the biggest, why the hell are you back now?

It's time to get these answers, I just have to ask without it sounding like an interrogation or make Topher even more uncomfortable.

I could also ease up on the defensive mode. There is no way they will feel welcome enough to open up and discuss it in front of me, and there is no way Topher will ask.

He's now playing with his napkin, folding it into some ornate design. Another sign he is out of his comfort zone.

I wonder if his parents know this about him. I wonder if they know him at all to know how torn up he is inside.

I doubt it. They wouldn't just rock up at his door unannounced if they knew him. Who does that? What a silly question. The same people that don't know how to put his needs before their own at all, as they have been MIA for eight years.

"And how about your bible studies?" Mary asks.

Topher looks down and shrugs. "I don't go to bible studies."

Mary looks to her husband, not impressed, then back to Topher. "That is no good, Tobias," she admonishes, ignoring the fact we established he no longer goes by that name.

"Topher," I remind her.

Her eyes land on me hard, but her smile is still perfectly in place. "I prefer Tobias. That was my father's name, God rest his soul."

Blah blah, no one cares what you prefer.

"Grandad is dead?" Topher asks, surprised. Anger boils deep inside. This woman is unbelievable. Is she that tone deaf she doesn't realise her son is struggling and maybe she should have given that information to him a little more tactfully?

"Oh yes, honey, a few months ago." She reaches for his hand. He freezes as she covers it with hers, stopping his origami and causing his skin to pale akin to a ghostly white. "He passed away peacefully in his home up north."

"Up north?" Why weren't there any attempts to have Topher moved into his care when his uncle went to jail?

"Queensland," Graham explains. That makes more sense. He lived in a different state.

"Oh ok. I am sorry for your loss," I say to Mary.

"Thank you. We didn't get to see each other a lot the last few years, but he was a good and fair man."

Topher slips his hand from under hers as the food pours out onto the table. It happens fast; one minute you're starving, the next minute there isn't an inch of the white table free as they spread our food out in front of us.

Topher and I always order up a storm, especially when we had the money to treat ourselves, but it kicked up five notches since Brian came here with us. He's a big boy, and he needs a lot of substance.

"What happened to your arm?" Mary asks, changing the subject.

Topher freezes mid spoon scoop of the E-shand Beef. It feels like moons ago that we were in the hospital, but it was only this morning.

"Oh, it was dumb. I accidentally hit the wine glass rack this morning, and the glass cut my arm."

"Wine?" Her forehead creases.

There goes me getting him drunk tonight. Miss judgy over here is worse than the cop sitting next to me. I look to Brian and he is happily filling up his plate.

He shrugs. "It was just an accident because I was nervous from the tests."

"Are you a big drinker?" Mary questions me.

"Huge," I deadpan, eyes fixed on her accusatory ones. "I love wine." I smile.

"Alcohol is the devil's nectar," she says.

"Huh?" I scrunch up my face. "Didn't Jesus turn water to wine? I'm confused." I am not religious, but I remember the pictures and all from religion classes at school.

"Oh sweetheart, that's not the purpose of that miracle." She shakes her head with a belligerent smile. "I take it you are not baptised, obviously, I should have picked that one up."

Obviously? What a bitch.

"Nope, my mother was too busy shoving needles in her arm to take me to church." I shrug. The table goes quiet. Brian's head whips to me. I know that was news to him, probably could have told him in a better environment, although it is something I don't enjoy talking about at all. "I take it you didn't know you left Topher with an alcoholic uncle?" I finish. Answer that one, then come and talk to me about my preference for a nice cab merlot.

I still feel Brian's gaze on me as Mary gasps. "That is uncalled for," she says. "And besides," she lifts her chin up, "we came back to get our son, but he was gone."

Bullshit.

"When?" I ask.

"You did?" Topher's body perks up. It's then I see the change in him. Hope. Hope that he wasn't left to fend for himself from the people that were meant to be his protectors.

She huffs and looks to Graham. "Oh god, uh, when was it?" She asks him for clarification. She doesn't wait, turning to me. "When we found out about the arrest. Fourteen. Yes. When Tobias was fourteen. When we enquired where he was, no one could help us."

"Really? I didn't know that." Topher looks at me. "Did you?"

Me? Why would I know that? Did he really think I

would withhold that piece of information from him?

"Of course not," I tell him.

"How did you two come to live together?" Graham adds to the questioning.

"I ran away from the group home I was in, and Elita rescued me from the thugs there. She let me live with her," Topher explains, now finding his voice.

"So, did you two already know each other? You are quite a bit older than him, how old were you when he came to live with you?" Graham continues as Mary tilts her head and she sits back in her chair.

"Nineteen," I answer.

"That sounds a little inappropriate,"

"Are you trying to insinuate that there was something going on with us? My god," I shake my head, "Topher isn't even stra- "

"Elita," Topher cuts me off.

"What?" I ask, truly confused. He shakes his head. Does he not want me to say he's gay?

Do they not know? How could they, he was only ten when they left? But why is he hiding it now? He's so proud of who he is and his sexuality; he has worked hard to get to this point. Overcome so much.

Mary shakes her head, "He was only a small boy, he should have been-"

"With his parents," I interrupt, "I agree. But he wasn't."

"Elita," Topher says, and I turn to him. His face tells it all, he's believing what they are saying, but there is no way they could have come back then.

I was in constant contact with his caseworker, she would have told me. I don't mention it to them because she let us fly under the radar once she realised he was in the best place he could be with me.

I close my mouth and sit up straight.

"Elita and Topher have a great relationship, and to me it seems like they are both lucky to have found each other." Brian rests his arm on the back of my chair. It's nice to have him in my corner.

"Well, I guess there is a lot to work out. It took us a long time to track you down," she says to Topher. "I am just so grateful and happy that I can see you again finally."

Topher chews on his bottom lip and nods.

She then turns to me. "I am sure you would feel the same if you were in my position."

"I would never be in your position."

Topher drops his head; his shoulders slump and I realise it's me now that is hurting him.

The table goes quiet, or merely I do. Topher seems to have found his voice and interacts more in the table conversation.

I retreat in my corner. Brian squeezes my shoulder and I look at him, he smiles, and I want to cry, but smile back instead.

"Excuse me." I stand and do something I thought I would never do in this restaurant. "I need the ladies' room." The bathroom is not the greatest here, but I will do anything right now to get out before one tear is shed.

I don't wait for a response; I am off and take a much-needed break from the shitstorm of a dinner.

It proved to be a big mistake.

"Yeah, I mean, I guess so," Topher answers as I take my seat again at the table.

"That's great." Mary claps and beams at Topher, then Graham. "It is going to be a wonderful weekend."

"Weekend?" I ask.

"It's going to be so great, you will love it," she continues before answering my question. "Yes, this weekend. Tobias has agreed to come away to a wellbeing retreat with us. Just what the doctor ordered after all your hard work studying."

I should have never gone to the bathroom. This does not sound good at all. I can't stop the nagging feeling that she is lying and they are hiding something. My worries will have to stay under wraps because the smile on Topher's face pulls on my heartstrings and I hope to Mary and Graham's God that I am wrong about this.

5

The Fire

THURSDAY

I wait at the beginning of the cul-de-sac, three houses away from the property they have sent me to repossess. Another quick glance at my watch. It's just turned 9am, and the locksmith is on the way. Just enough time to make the call I've been planning all night.

I flick through my contacts until I hit her name. Topher's old caseworker, Cindy. It has been years since I last spoke to her. She was definitely one of the good ones, even though she didn't follow procedure to the letter. She did what was best for Topher, allowing him to stay with me, and for that I will always be grateful.

She will know if his parents ever tried to make contact. I just can't believe that if they did, she wouldn't have told me. That was the plan. If they came back, it meant her ringing me to give me a heads up first. I was barely an adult myself. Even then, I knew Topher should be with his parents. If they were fit to be parents, of course.

I press call and place the phone to my ear.

"The number you have called has been disconnected. You have not been charged for this call." The robot lady on the other end of the phone tells me.

Well, that isn't great. I can try DCP where she worked, maybe she just changed her number.

Once I find the department's number online, I hit call and remember the long wait times I used to experience. That was one of the reasons Cindy gave me her mobile number.

A five-minute wait and another robot answers my call. This one prompts me through the menu and again after another ten minutes a human answer the phones.

"Hello, Department for Child Protection, how can I help you?" a woman says.

"Hi, my name is Elita, I was looking to speak with Cindy Turner?" A white van with a big key printed on it drives past and parks in the property's driveway. Damn, he's here.

"Sorry," she says as I pack up my drink bottle and folder into my backpack while I listen. "No one works here by that name. Can I help you?"

What? She left? If it suited anyone for that job, it was Cindy. I don't blame her though; it would be one of the toughest jobs in the world, being a social worker. Now I'm screwed. I try desperately to filter my brain for any other names that I can remember.

"Does Renata still work there?" I hope I have the name right; I remember Cindy being close with her. I get out of my car and slam the door closed, walking straight towards Mark, the locksmith.

"Um, yes, Renata does. I can leave a message with her. She should be in soon," the woman says.

Great, I give the woman my details. Mark nods his head at me as I stop in front of him. I return the gesture while saying my goodbyes and hanging up. Hopefully Renata will help me when she gets in.

"Sorry I'm late, I forgot to plug my phone in to charge last night and it died on the way. Lucky I have the best memory in the world." He taps his head after he sees me put the phone in my pocket.

"No problem, I had some calls to make, anyway. I got a charger in the car if you need it."

"Yeah, that would be great, I'll fire it up once we're inside," he says. "You wanna do the breaking in today?"

"You know I do." I beam up to him. Mark has been giving me lessons and my own B&E kit. What we're doing is not illegal, for Mark anyway, since they have hired our firm to assist with seizing the house. Unfortunately, the owners have not made contact or paid any repayments for seven months and the bank has had enough.

We need to break in with minimal damage, change all outside locks, and give the new keys to the bank. While Mark does that, I do an inventory of what is in the house. It's going to be a busy day.

By the time we get inside, I feel like a real badass. There is no mess and with no accidents, even impressing Mark. He stays at the front and works to change the front door for our safety. Just in case the owner, tenants, or whoever has a key comes in while we are working.

The house is run down. After a quick look around, I find the kitchen at the back. I was wrong. The inventory won't take long at all. The furniture is sparse, with a metal dining table and two mismatched chairs pushed up against the wall in the small space. I drop my bag on the table, open it up and pull out my folder to begin. There's a constant buzzing sound, it grinds my nerves already. I can thank Topher for that and that stupid prank he pulled on me with the Annoy-a-tron last year. The evil device that emits out frequency sounds that can't be found. Three months I heard an on and off buzzing sound in our old apartment, even after the truth came out. It was one of the driving forces behind us having to leave. Not from the sound since it was all from this microchip device, but from me losing it at the landlord because he couldn't fix it. Which ended up being because there was nothing to fix. Didn't I feel a fool once all was revealed. How? Topher sending me a link to his online chronicles on me going crazy. He built up a following, too, that little punk.

This sound is different though. It's constant, but still nerve-racking. Possibly the fridge? A shiver runs through me as I walk towards it. Please don't be filthy. But when I walk towards the fridge, the sound doesn't get louder. The moment of truth. Opening a rundown fridge in a derelict dirty house. This is so gross. I open it and the light does not go on. In fact, the fridge is not even on. Huh? Does anyone live here at all?

I wonder where that noise is coming from then? I race and collect my folder and pen, determined to find the noise and get this job done.

Starting at the front of the house, I open all the doors to see what is inside. Finding one room with a mattress and dirty brown quilt on the floor, the other empty except with black rubbish bags filled with rubbish, I presume. The carpet looks like they haven't been cleaned in a very long time, with what looks like leaves and debris from outside filtering through the house.

But there is a door that's locked. I look back at the other door handles; they are different. They have replaced the doorknob in front of me with one that requires a key.

Curiosity peaked, I run back to my bag to get my lock kit. I carefully pry apart the door frame and fiddle with the old credit card until the lock pops open.

With a whoosh, the waft of marijuana assaults my senses and the bright hydro lights up ahead present ten huge plants. With the size of the plants and the buds on them, it looks like they almost had enough money to pay off the debt to the bank.

"Holy shit," Mark says as he comes up behind me.

"Yep, it is going to be a long ass day." I pull my phone from the back pocket to call this into the police.

~

It hasn't been long since I made the call to the police, but already I have finished the rest of my report on the contents in the house. Mark and I got our story straight, he was the one to break into the room, we even went as far as to put his prints on where I did. How I ended up with a cop is beyond me. I can already see Brian shaking his head, if I tell him, of course.

A sudden vibration comes from my back pocket and then my ringtone. Pulling it out, I see an unknown caller.

"Hello, Elita speaking," I answer as I walk straight out to the front of the house for privacy, hoping it's the social worker.

"Hi, it's Renata. I'm returning your call. Is this Elita? Elita Machiavelli?"

"Uh, yeah. It is."

"Oh yes, I remember you. They said you were calling for Cindy?"

"Yeah. I was told she doesn't work there anymore," I

say now pacing out on the footpath.

"She doesn't. She moved to Western Australia with her husband," Renata says.

"Husband? Oh, wow, I didn't even know she got married." It's not like we were that close that she would have invited me to her wedding, so it isn't too surprising I didn't know.

"Yeah, and she just literally had a baby. A little girl." Renata beams and her infectious positiveness hits me smack in the head. I remember Renata was Cindy's best friend, I even met them one time for coffee. "It was definitely a blast from the past when I saw your name on my message list. Is everything ok?"

"Yeah, it is. I just needed to confirm something with Cindy about a case from back then."

"Anything I can help with?" she asks. Even though I know they were close, I can't guarantee she was in the loop of our agreement, so I am not willing to go there yet.

"Actually, there is. Do you know how to get in touch with her? I tried her number, but it was disconnected."

"Oh yeah, when she left, the number was too involved with the department, so she changed it for a fresh start. I would give you her number, but I will have to check with her first."

Yes, she still talks to her. I feel like doing a happy dance.

Mark comes up from behind me, looking like he has

something to say.

"That would be great, can you just give me one sec?" I cover the phone with one hand away from my ear and wait for Mark to talk.

"You got that charger?" he asks.

I nod and pull out the keys in my other pocket, throwing it to him. "Can I give you my number and if she can call me back as soon as possible, that would be great?" I continue as he runs off to my car.

"Of course. I'm not sure when she will get back to you, though. She was pretty wrecked when I last spoke to her. You know, newborn and all."

Nope, no idea what that is like, but I agree. "Yeah, no worries, I get it. If you could tell her it's about Topher's parents, that would be great." My foot hits something on the pavement and I trip. Looking down, a white cable in the middle of the footpath grove looks to be the culprit.

That's strange.

Mark runs past me again, heading inside to charge his phone so he can tell everyone we are in a grow house. I shake my head at the turn of events and shouldn't be surprised, as these things always seem to happen to me.

"I can do that, not a problem. Is there anything else you need?" she asks. I follow the white cable from the footpath leading all the way to the electricity pole.

"No, thank you. And thank you for your help, I really appreciate it." My head lifts higher and higher up the pole.

"Of course. Cindy had your name on our hotlist to be put straight through. I will make sure I pass the message on," she assures.

My eyes hit the end of the cable that hangs off jumper cables and exposed wire.

"Awesome, thanks. Sorry, I gotta go," I say as I realise they are stealing power, and doesn't look safe at all. "Thanks for your help Renata, hope you have a great day," I rush out.

"You, too. Goodbye, Elita," she says as I hang up.

I don't wait as I run to stop Mark from plugging in his phone. But as soon as I make it into the kitchen, he flicks the switch and I am too late. He flies back with a loud cry and all the lights and power go off.

He sits up on his bum, hair raised four inches above his head.

"OH MY GOD, are you ok?" I run up but don't touch him, who knows if he still has currents running through him.

His head bobs around and if we were in a cartoon, he would have a string of stars floating about his head.

"What's that smell?" he asks.

"Uh, what smell?" Crap, now I have to call an ambulance. But he's right, there is a smell. Like burnt rubber, or...

I turn behind me; the outlet is on fire.

Oh fuck. "Get up." I pull Mark.

He is dazed and absolutely confused. Loud police sirens from the front blare and it's music to my ears. I help Mark to his feet and we make our way outside as fast as we can.

I throw the door open and see none other than Brian and Max, his partner, jump out of their car.

Great. Out of everyone, it had to be Brian. He sees me holding up Mark and breaks into a sprint.

"What's happened?" Brian asks as he assesses every inch of me.

"Fire," Mark says.

"What?" Brian booms.

Here we go, another one I will not be able to live down.

~

I open the big red door of our apartment completely and utterly exhausted. At least I'm not Brian, who is back at the station. Stuck having to write out his report of this fuck up of a day.

I drop my things on the couch as I make my way through the open plan level, looking up and seeing Topher's light on.

I need a shower and food and alcohol. The first two I skip and grab a bottle of wine with two glasses and make my way upstairs to his room.

When I walk in, he's packing. My stomach sinks.

"Hey." I hold up the wine.

"Hey." He smiles. "Rough day?" he asks, nodding to the wine.

I just nod and pour a glass. "You want one?" I sit on the corner of his bed.

"Definitely." He plops down next to me. He screws up his face leaning into me sniffing. "What is that smell?"

"Weed maybe, could be smoke, too." I sniff, trying to see which one is stronger.

"Uh, what?" His eyes go wide.

I run down the story to him, minus the attempted contact of Cindy.

"That sucks, I wish I was there," he says.

I laugh. "Of course you do."

I focus back on the bag he is packing. "So you are really going, huh?" I nod to it.

He looks down to his glass and nods. "Why, do you think I shouldn't?" He looks up at me with Bambi eyes.

No, I don't but I don't know if it's my place to say it. "I don't know. I think maybe it's a bit soon."

His body falls and he shrugs. "They really seem like they want to make up for everything."

"Maybe," I say. "A weekend, though? It's a bit fast."

He looks to me. "It sounds like I might like it."

"What is it? Is it a religious thing?" I pray he is not walking into some sort of cult.

"Shit, no. I already told them I'm not into that anymore, and they seemed fine with it," he says. "It's a wellness and mindfulness retreat. Sounds like a lot of relaxing to me."

I nod and bite my inner cheek. That feeling I get when I sense bullshit has not settled since they resurfaced.

"Seriously, it isn't anything to do with religion. They promised," he says. I nod again and want to pat myself on the back for not rolling my eyes. "Come with us tomorrow then."

"What's tomorrow?" I frown.

"It's a seminar with the guy who runs it. I think his name is Lincoln or something. Come and see for yourself," he says, but I get the feeling he's asking me to come for support, not just to suss out this seminar.

"Of course I'll come. I think I need some wellness in my life." I smile at him.

He returns it with a weak one. "Can I ask you something?"

"Of course, anything."

"Can you be nice and give them a chance tomorrow?" He gives me the look again.

Even though it's the last thing in the world I want to do, I agree. "Yeah, I will be Susie Sunshine."

This makes him laugh.

I take a long drink of my wine. Tomorrow I'm going to be watching them like a hawk.

6

The Seminar

FRIDAY

Hoards of people are streaming into the waiting area outside the main arena of the Adelaide Convention Centre on the banks of the Torrens River in the city.

They pack the large open foyer with what looks to be thousands waiting to see this Lincoln Jones character. The buzz in the room is electric, bubbling with anticipation. Music blasts from the speakers with actual cheerleaders performing on the floor lifting the energy, encouraging people to yell and cheer as they go past. It's infectious as Topher is already jumping up and down with excitement.

I hate it already.

So much for wellness and mindfulness. I am getting a headache and I just got here. And is that a fire breather? The man just in front of us with piercings blows a stick.

Fire blazes out and the surrounding crowd claps.

I have no problems with a circus, but I brought my goddamn notebook in my backpack, not peanuts. I thought this was a seminar.

Topher grabs a hold of my arm. "I see them there, let's go." He pulls me toward his waiting parents. "So not what I expected, is it?" he bellows.

I plaster on a smile. "Not at all."

He swings his head at me but sees my smile and relaxes. I have already promised multiple times this morning not to be a bitch, even after I paid the five hundred bloody dollars to come.

There are five hundred things I would rather spend that money on. Especially after the money I dropped on my new car and the advance on my rent.

Lincoln Jones better be worth it.

Mary and Graham spot us through the crowd. She does not even try to hide the disappointment at seeing me. Not going to bite on that. I made a promise.

"Hi!" I call out when we stop. My pitch way too high and too over eager. The fake smile already hurts my cheeks. Even Topher looks at me, surprised with my perkiness.

Mary takes a moment to recover, but as a well-trained bullshit artist herself, her smile reaches from ear to ear. "Oh hello, Elita. I wasn't aware you were coming today?"

Be nice, I remind myself.

"Topher invited me last night, and I bought a ticket."

I glance quickly around. "This is amazing, so much excitement." I beam at them.

This shakes the stick from her ass out. "Isn't it?" She reaches and grabs my hand. All my instincts are screaming at me to rip my hands away, but I smile harder, my cheeks almost up to my eyes. The more I talk about the things she likes, the more she will let her guard down. "This is just the beginning. Lincoln is amazing." She turns her attention to Topher, dropping my hands. "Honey, you have my number, you should have let me know, I could have gotten you an extra ticket."

It will be a cold day in hell before I take a thing from her.

"Oh, sorry I didn't even think to," Topher says. But his eyes are still scanning the crowd at the copious amounts of stimuli that are being thrown in our faces.

"Next time," she boasts, looking back at me. "We know Lincoln quite well. So we can get a little discount."

"Is that a tiger?" Topher shouts, grabbing my arm again, pointing.

Yes, that is a tiger. Just casually sitting in the corner with what looks like a very underwhelming chain that is the only thing stopping me from being its next meal. I take a small step behind Mary; he can have her first.

Graham chuckles and slaps Topher on the back. "Yes, trust me, son. This is just the beginning."

"Look how trained it is. The guy is hardly even worried," Topher says.

"Not at all," Graham says. "From my understanding, the tiger is new. That's the whole point, if you will it you can control it."

Uh, does he not see the red glassy eyes of the drugged-out tiger? If that doesn't give it away, then the drool coming from the tiger's mouth where its face is limp and droopy to one side should. Either way, I still stay behind Mary, maybe I can will that into fruition.

"No way," Topher says in awe. This time I roll my eyes. Luckily, no one sees it.

"THE TIME HAS COME!" An ominous voice sounds over the audio system. All activities end abruptly. The music, the dancers, the fire breather.

The doors to the venue open, white smoke and cinematic music flow out. Overly dramatic if you ask me, but it's being lapped up. The amazement and intrigue mirrored in faces all around me.

Here we go, let's meet this Lincoln Jones.

~

My leg won't stop bouncing up and down as I wait in the red allocated seat. It has been close to ten minutes and still no Lincoln Jones. The same thing happens at a concert when they set the mood and suspense. I get it at a concert. Everyone is aware they are about to witness a performance, but this seminar is sixty minutes and I plan to be back in my car in sixty-five. It better not go over.

Where the hell is he?

The music stops. A white screen comes down from the ceiling, coming to a stop before the projector shines an image of a cloudy sky with rays of sunshine streaming out from it.

"What if I told you everything you need is already within yourself?" A smooth American male's voice announces and cheers filter through the arena.

"Watch and visualise, find what is important to you. What do you want? Love? Happiness? Wealth?" The voice continues.

The video now plays in front of us. Families walking along stunning beaches, a well-dressed man in a suit stepping off of a private plane. On and on, imagery that portrays what most people view as success flash before our eyes.

"What if I told you, you are one step closer to achieving all of this and more?" The voice continues.

I'd say you're a nutcase, I answer in my head.

A loud bang has me jump in my seat. I'm not alone; the shock makes people gasp and sit on the edge of their seat. A spotlight shines on the back door. It swings open. The crowd comes to life. Lincoln Jones runs out, the audience is cheering, and it looks as though he is doing a couple of laps around the stage, running around and encouraging more.

What a douche.

He stops in the centre and raises his hands to the sky, slowly bringing them down, the audience hushing following his directions.

He brings the microphone from his hand to his mouth.

"I want to tell you a story," he starts. "About a little five-year-old boy on a ranch in the mid-west of the United States of America and his quest for enlightenment." He already has lost my interest. What little boy even knows what the word enlightenment is?

As he continues with what I guess is his life story or even completely made up, his voice goes from high to low, in a rhythmic dynamic pace. I survey the room. The audience is captivated, but that was already a given from the theatrics outside and his showmanship. But now they are nodding along, listening to how this troubled boy could rise above adversity to become who he is today. Master to his own destiny.

What I find interesting is the dozen or more men and women standing at the end of the aisles. All wearing blue shirts and all with their eyes fixed on the crowd, scanning.

What are they looking for?

I check my aisle and see a woman that has her eyes on me. She raises her eyebrows and smiles, pointing back to the stage and then to her eyes for me to face forward.

I feel like a scolded child. With a slow nod, I leave the

woman to her business and return my attention to the man in front of me.

"And I want to teach you. I will hand you the key," he finishes.

The crowd erupts.

"We are in an age now. An age where science has now caught up with spirituality," he says. "Are you excited?" he yells out.

The crowd's roar answers his questions.

"For real wealth and abundance, for life altering and soulful love. What if I told you the only person who can give it to you, is you?" Lincoln Jones strides up towards the front of the stage.

I don't get it. Is he telling us this is true? Dude just spit it out, he has been dribbling the same crap the entire opening.

"You." He points at someone in the front row. "You." He points to someone else in the crowd. "You." He points again, each time the applause gets louder. "All of you." He finishes waving his arms over the entire crowd.

I take a deep breath in and look at Topher, he must feel my gaze and he looks back to me, his brows furrowed just like mine.

What a relief. He, too, can see the sheer lunacy of this. He shrugs and looks dubiously back at Lincoln Jones.

Sucked in Mary, hopefully Lincoln continues to make a fool of himself and I can convince Topher to skip the weekend retreat. Maybe I will even offer to have a LAN party with him for his choice of computer game this weekend. That is more his speed.

I relax into the chair.

"Now let's all try this. Close your eyes," he directs the room. "Come on. Everyone. Close your eyes."

Harmonic and serene sounds waft through the speakers, as everyone does as he says. He drops the high notes from his pitch. "Now, I want everyone to sit very, very still. And concentrate. Visualise what your ideal life would be like with an abundance in health, wealth, relationships, happiness and spirituality," each word spoken slowly and hypnotically, "the five pillars and the five peaks we all strive for."

I turn to Topher and he has his eyes closed; I sigh and lay my head back, closing my eyes. After the events of yesterday I just hope I don't nod off, I'm still exhausted plus having a restless sleep. That woman that was watching me before will probably lose it if I snore.

~

The last twenty minutes have cost me one hundred and sixty-six dollars. How do I know this? Because I have had an abundance of time to sit and calculate every dollar. Sitting in this uncomfortable chair with my eyes closed, waiting until that nut job says we can open them again. He has been spewing garbage in his rhythmic annoying voice, on and off the entire time. Apart from a few whispers here and there, the audience sits quietly. And if there was a noise or someone talking, the blue Smurfs that watch over the audience were onto them quickly, I saw two being escorted out of the room. I wanted to raise my hand and yell, "Pick me."

"Slowly, open your eyes and come back to me," Lincoln Jones finally says. Life slowly comes back into the room. Whispers turned to chattering and energy buzzes through the air.

"Now let's get to work." He claps his hands. "I need volunteers, anyone. Raise your hands and one of my Spirt Crew may very well select you."

Hands fly up, raised high. Mary has her hand raised, beaming with excitement. I sink in my chair. Please, please don't pick her. The Smurfs pick off people one by one until the woman who had been watching me earlier squeezes past me to select Mary from her chair.

"This should be interesting," I say to Topher as we watch the chosen five make their way on the stage.

"Well, I didn't mind the last part, it was relaxing. Kind of like meditation," he says. I give him a side eye and he laughs.

I scoff, "More like his attempt at hypnosis."

"Elita," he warns.

"Fine, fine." I settle back, eyes forward. Ready for this

guy to parade around the stage again.

What he does, though, leaves me speechless. One by one, he goes through the five guests asking them to reveal deeply personal and troubling details. Things that clearly should only be discussed in the safety of a professional physiatrist. Child abuse, affairs, self image. He probes and pushes until it forces them to reveal whatever he deems as the ticket. A ticket being one of the many pieces of baggage we carry around.

I feel uncomfortable and icky as I watch. Until they call Mary up for her turn. I lean forward. This shall be compelling.

"Would you like to introduce yourself?" Lincoln Jones asks her.

She steps closer to the microphone stand. "My name is Mary Palmer."

"Hello Mary." Lincoln turns to the crowd. "Everyone, welcome Mary." The audience obediently claps. She gleams at the spotlight as she flicks her hair, loving the attention. "Now Mary, tell us all something true. Something that hinders you and keeps you up at night."

She takes a long inhale in. "Well, I have always been very religious." She looks to Lincoln, and he nods for her to continue. "But it sent me following someone that took my husband and I's faith and used it to their advantage." That is news. So she has always been gullible and taken for a ride easily. Doesn't she see she's just jumped ship from one bullshit artist to the other?

"And it keeps me up at night, sometimes," she pauses and looks to the crowd then back to Lincoln, building up the suspense. Mary leans forward to the microphone. "I even questioned... if there even is a God." Both hands fly over her mouth as she shakes her head. "I can't believe I even said that."

The crowd cheers at her breakthrough.

"Mary, I can't keep going, I have to be real here," Lincoln pipes in. "When I look at you, that is not what I see."

"It's not?" She turns, stunned to Lincoln.

"No Mary, no it is not. I look at you and I see shame." The crowd draws a collective gasp, but I smile, the first genuine smile. Leaning forward, I finally want to hear what he has to say. "What makes you so full of shame Mary?"

"Excuse me?" Her voice quivers.

I even feel a tad bit bad for her. Being called out in front of thousands of people. But the moment passes quickly, and I am captivated waiting for her response.

"You can continue lying to yourself and to me, or you can look inside, grab that ticket and tear it up." He turns to the crowds. "Tear it up. Tear it up," he chants in the microphone and the room, just like good little sheep, they all chant along with him.

"I abandoned my son, and he hates me." Tears stream from her face as the room goes quiet.

I look at Topher, and his face says he's no longer

having fun. He is anxious and pale. What a selfish woman. I don't think I will ever stop being amazed at how some people should just not have children.

"There it is. The shame. Everyone, can you see the shame Mary is pouring out?" Again the room cheers.

What the hell is wrong with people? Is he even licensed to do this? Surely there must be some degrees listed under his achievements somewhere. I pick up the flyer again and quickly scan for something of the sort.

"Now it is out there, Mary. Maybe one day he will be brought back into your life, ask and you shall receive."

"He already is," she says into the microphone.

"He is?" Lincoln booms. "Mary. Don't tell me he is here," he says, looking out to the audience.

Wait a minute. Didn't she say they were close, isn't this something he might already know? Especially since he is going away with her and I would assume him this weekend for his retreat.

"Where is he, can he come up? Mary, what is his name?" he says.

My mouth drops open. Oh shit.

"Tobias," she says.

I growl. I actually growl.

I turn to Topher. "You don't have to go."

He looks at me, eyes bugging out of his head, the crowd chanting Tobias. It happens quick, the blue Smurf has already started towards us, and I want to karate chop her and run Topher out of here to safety.

He stands.

Topher gets to his feet, his dad patting him on the back for encouragement. A lump forms in my throat as I watch him being led to the front of the stage.

The sinking feeling in the pit of my stomach is back. This is not good. This is really not good.

7

The Ticket

FRIDAY

The stage seems smaller, Topher is standing in between his mother and Lincoln Jones at the microphone stand.

Thousands of eyes are fixed on him. Normally Topher would be in his element right now, but he looks like he could be sick at any moment.

The crowd's applause slowly fades as Lincoln Jones brings the hand-held microphone to his lips.

"Thank you, young man, for being so brave to come up here today."

The crowd cheers, and Topher stays silent at the stand.

"Tobias," Lincoln says, "now we all are waiting to hear what your thoughts are about what your mother has just discovered."

Topher looks between his mother and Lincoln Jones,

shrugging. "I'm not sure," he answers.

"Ok, well that is why you are here. It's ok to not have all the answers right now. That is why I'm here. To teach you."

The crowd cheers.

"Mary has just told everyone how she left her son to follow a religious pursuit and that she feels as though you hate her. Do you hate her?" he asks.

Who is this guy to probe so deep into someone's life like this, and that damn woman, how can she think putting her son in this situation is the right thing to do?

"Sometimes," Topher says, "but I love my life and if she hadn't left, I would never have been where I am now, so not really."

Good on you, Topher, tell them to shove it.

I smile.

"Do you?" Lincoln raises his brow. "Or are you pretending you love your life?" He then turns his attention to the crowd. "Everyone can learn something from this bright young man. He can stand here next to his mother who abandoned him, and still says he loves his life. So courageous and strong."

He shakes his head in disbelief, turning to Topher. "How old are you, son?"

Urgh, he is not your son. I've always been protective of Topher, but I have never felt so concerned about his safety. This overwhelming sense of darkness, looms. The same feeling that had me hiding as a little girl. I can not shake the feeling that he is in danger. But the more Lincoln Jones is praising him, the taller Topher stands and the more confidence he embodies. This is worse, this means he is listening to this bullshit.

"I have just turned eighteen."

"Excellent, you are now a man and it is up to you right here and right now, to look to the woman who gave birth to you and tell her you forgive her."

Mary's hands fly to her face, fingers covering her lips. She waits for the holy grail of words that should not be given so easily to her.

"Um," Topher's confidence takes a hit.

"Or should we stay here and throw stones? Up to you. We can sit here and let Mary know how disgusting and ashamed she should be." He points to Mary.

Topher's mouth falls open.

"Tell her how she should have her womb removed. Because she never should've been allowed to have a child."

Mary gasps.

My mouth even gapes open. How harsh, even I haven't had that thought of Mary, or even my own mother.

"I don't," Topher shakes his head, looking at his mum.

The camera now has picked up a feed projecting Topher's face on the large screen behind him.

"Really, you don't?" He shrugs. "It doesn't look that way, otherwise you would ease her pain. Is it because you like it?"

I grab the armrests and clench them tight, grounding me right here so I do not make a scene.

"Of course not. No." He shakes his head fervently.

"You 'don't?" he asks once more.

"No." This time Topher's voice is firm.

"Then why do you want to punish her?"

"I don't." Topher raises his shoulder, dropping his head. Clearly he feels threatened. Why does he keep pushing?

The more Lincoln Jones attacks Mary, the more her tears are falling and Topher steps closer to her.

"Then tell her. Tell her you forgive her." He turns to the crowd. "Come on, everyone, let's help him. Forgive her. Forgive her."

Here he goes again with the chanting and peer pressure from everyone.

"Forgive her," rings through the arena.

The lights go darker and the spotlight falls on both Topher and Mary.

Mary steps to the microphone. "You don't have to do anything you aren't ready to, honey," she reassures Topher.

Awes ring through the crowd.

Topher shakes his head as he steps up to the stand, Mary taking a step back.

"If there was ever a strong man, Tobias, he is you. You have the answers. You have the courage. You have the power."

The crowd rips into cheer.

"Do it," he yells into the microphone.

"I forgive you," Topher says into the microphone, Mary drops to her knees crying.

Just like a grand finale of a home renovation game show, the roof drops coloured confetti down.

Everywhere, all over the stage, all over Topher bending down to console his mother, over the audience who are all standing and cheering.

"Thank you everyone," Lincoln Jones says.

I jump to my feet as I have lost sight of Topher.

The music gets louder.

"Remember, it is YOU. It is in everyone. Just like Tobias, we are all the masters to our own destiny. Tear up your ticket and find it yourself."

I have to jump to see as Topher helps his mother to her feet, a Smurf is there helping as they are being ushered to the back door of the stage.

"And remember, we have a range of courses to suit everyone's level. Ask a spirit crew and thank you, Adelaide, for coming today."

No one is making a move to go, everyone still reeling from the breakthrough and the show.

I don't wait, my feet run to the exit. I need to get Topher out of this and take him home so he can have time to think about what has just happened before he has to leave tonight.

After what I just saw, I also need to find a way to convince him that this is a terrible idea.

~

Even though I'm the first out, I don't know where to go. I look around, try to find the entrance to the back. Try to see where he would come out from, but nothing.

So I wait.

I wait when people flock out of the arena, talking and holding onto each other in excitement.

"Wasn't that amazing?" one person says.

"Did you hear what he said?" another says.

"Did you see what that guy did?"

With every comment, my blood boils hotter and thicker, but still no Topher. The crowd dissipates, and I am left standing on the sidewalk until I hear my name called.

"Elita." I turn and Topher's running to me.

But behind him next to a large travel bus is his mother, father, Lincoln Jones and an entire clan of Smurfs.

He comes racing to me.

"Are you ready?" I ask him, wanting to get the hell out of there.

"Oh my god, how amazing was that?" His eyes dilate, the adrenaline still radiating from his body, he beams a smile that has me swallowing a lump of anxiety.

I say nothing.

"I have to be quick, we're leaving right now." He looks back and Lincoln Jones waves him to come back. Topher over-eagerly returns the wave.

"What do you mean? You don't even have your clothes here." I try to bring him back to reality. His clothes, laptop, everything he was planning to take is back at the warehouse.

"I don't need them," he declares.

"What the hell are you talking about?" I say as I peer over his shoulder, watching Mary talking into Lincoln Jones's ear.

"Mum said I can get things on the way; it will be better anyway. Go in completely fresh."

"Oh, did she," I say, jaw clenched.

"Elita?" Topher whines. "You promised."

I let out a long deep breath; I promised. What am I meant to do anyway, grab him by the ear and drag him into the car?

Wait a minute, how bad would that be?

I shake my head and let go of that idea. "Look, just this whole thing is a bit—" I pause, thinking of the right word.

"I know it's a bit out there, but I really feel like I can learn a lot. And you said you wanted to see if it was a religious cult thing, and it's not, right?"

I rub my face with my hands before answering. "No,

it doesn't sound like it." I had to admit it.

"TOBIAS!" Lincoln Jones calls out. "The bus is leaving."

"Why the fuck are they calling you that? Why don't they listen when you tell them your name?"

He sighs, head dropping. "I don't know, whatever, I will tell them when we're there again."

I hate making him feel this way; he was so full of life when he came to me. "I will see you Monday, ok?" He looks up at me and plasters on a smile.

"Ok, Monday." My shoulders slump. There is nothing I can do.

Like a switch, life comes back into him. "Monday, and - " he walks backwards, "enjoy your two-day boink fest with lover boy."

This makes me laugh.

"Love you, Sunshine," he calls out as he runs towards the closing doors of the bus.

"Love you, too," I call out, but I'm not sure he hears it as the doors close behind him.

~

I slam the last glass on the table before dropping in my seat. "And then he just left," I finish explaining what happened today to Brian.

Brian has already started dishing out the food on his

plate, his tired and hungry eyes fixed on the job. "Well, hopefully he comes back all fresh and ready for his holidays."

That's it. That is all he has to say about the ridiculous day. "I told you about the drugged-up tiger, yeah?" Maybe he didn't hear that bit.

He chuckles, "Yep, fire breather, cheerleaders, all of it. Actually, the last one doesn't sound too bad." He shoves a piece of broccoli in his mouth.

"Ha, ha, ha." I roll my eyes, which just makes his laugh turn deeper. "See, it isn't even the girls in short skirts. That I can understand if Topher was chasing after cute girls. But it was just the stupid show that pressured him into forgiving his mum."

"Is that a bad thing?" he asks.

"Yes." I put a piece of grilled chicken on my plate. Yuck, I hate eating so clean and healthy, but we used up Brian's cheat day when we had dinner with Topher's parents.

He raises a brow at me. "Most people would think that was a good thing, Elita."

"Well, I am not most people, obviously."

"That's for sure," he says. "I'm still feeling the effects from yesterday."

"Huh, we didn't even have sex yesterday. You were at work all day."

He laughs, "There won't be a day on this Earth you

will hear me complain about the lingering after effects of sex with you."

I smile proudly.

"And yes, exactly. I was at work all day yesterday. Remember why that was?"

I close my mouth with a pop and sink into my chair.

"You're still famous at the station from your pimp arrest, let alone setting a drug crop on fire."

"I didn't set it on fire." He doesn't even know about the B&E that I did. I fill my mouth with food, so I don't get myself in anymore trouble.

"I'm playing. But seriously, it was a long night to wrap up that job, but at the end, turns out they linked it to Petrov." His face hardens, and his eyes go dark just like it does every time he says that name.

"Really?" I wouldn't have thought from the name on the file they linked it to the Russians that were responsible for what happened to his sister. This is big. "So what now, can you look more into him?" He's been busting his ass to make detective so that he can really go after Vlad. Maybe this is what he needs to get a jump start on it. In six months, I have only seen tears in his eyes once. That was talking about the death of his sister. The reason he became a cop.

"Nothing." He cracks his neck and shakes off the darkness. "They took me off the case because of what happened and our connection." He continues eating.

I sink lower, my hand falling limp, the fork dinging on my plate as I let it rest. "I didn't know, I'm sorry."

"Obviously," he says. "Babe, don't worry about it. There will be more times." His smile is weak.

This is crushing, and I'm the cause. How can I possibly make it up to him?

"You know what I really don't understand, though," he asks, "is why we spent the first hour talking about some stupid seminar that is nothing to worry about, when we still haven't talked about what you said at dinner. The night with Topher's parents." His eyes fix on me.

"What did I say?" I frown. I know I said a lot, I was an outright bitch. He will have to be way more specific than that.

"About your mother," he answers.

"Oh," I clear my throat. I know what he's talking about now.

"How come you never told me about the drugs?" His voice is soft, the hardness from earlier gone. Even with the change in demeanour, I don't want to go there at all.

"Because it doesn't matter." I shrug, hoping he will drop it.

"It doesn't work like that, babe. We both have to open up to each other. You know all my shit, I want to be there for yours, too."

"You are. But that shit is in the past, Brian. I don't want to go there. I just filed it in a box called Nothing

Important and I let it sit there." Why would I give her more power over me by festering in the unfairness of life? I don't see the point.

"Is that the same box that explains the tattoo you never want to talk about?"

My hand goes to the back of my neck, the raised scar from a tattoo I never remember getting and wouldn't want to even if I did. This was during my time with her. I fix my hair to make sure it's covered again.

"It's all in the past, what does it matter?" I swallow the lump in my throat.

"Well, maybe the box needs to be cleared because I think it may cloud your judgement on Topher reuniting with his parents."

My eyebrows raise so high I'm surprised they don't jump off my face and hit the roof. "Um, no, I don't think so." I cross my arms

"Really. Then why are you so against Topher and his parents working it out?"

"Of course I'm not," I frown. "I want Topher to have as much people in his life that love him as possible. I just think they're up to something. And that cult they brought with them. They better get ready cause I'm onto them." This conversation is pissing me off, so I decide I've had enough to eat and start packing up my plate.

"Elita." Brian reaches for my hand, taking it in his. "Ok, how about this." I sigh and sit back down again. "Let me do a few checks on them and if it all comes back clear, you promise you will let it go."

I'm about to tell him hell no, then he drops the kicker. "I can't afford to get kicked off another case right now, and I can see your mind in overdrive. This is important to me, I just can't get into any more shit at work."

The wind gets kicked out of me as guilt has me back in the chair with my eyes closed. Is Brian right? Am I letting my drama impede Topher having his family in his life?

I don't know, but I know that it's crucial Brian makes detective. I can't, no, I will not be the reason that doesn't happen.

"Ok," I say opening my eyes and looking into his. "If you look into Lincoln Jones and Topher's parents and it's all ok, I'll drop it."

"Promise?" he asks.

"Promise." At that moment, I truly believed those words.

8

The Call

SUNDAY

I lost an entire day. Wasted in bed, crippled with the worst headache I have ever had my entire life.

The good news is, the pummelling of the shower in the room next to me doesn't make my head explode. It's safe to say the debilitating pain that I felt yesterday has finally subsided.

Still, I lay here in bed with my eyes closed, too scared to open them. The memories of the migraine have me expecting immense pain when I do.

I peek one eye open and the familiar black iron lampshade fixed to my ceiling welcomes me back to the land of the living. The other eye opens faster and after a few quick blinks, I lift my head off the pillow.

No immense pain.

That's a good sign. I shuffle up, my body still aches and feels worn, but I still manage a smile when Brian walks in with his towel wrapped around his waist. His tattoos on full display.

"Hey, you're up." He walks to his small area in the corner of my room where his things live.

"Barely," I grumble. Whatever hit me the night Topher left has gone away. It's a start. My body still feels as though I've run a marathon and my head is heavy. But I can sit up now.

"How are you feeling? The headache gone?" He whips the towel off as he changes.

"Yeah, finally." I was fine before I went to bed. Yes, stressed and still reeling from the seminar and our dinner. Plus, I tossed and turned all night. So when I finally fell asleep, whatever I dreamt must have been a nightmare. I woke up dripping in sweat and with a start.

"Good, because I was worried." He comes and sits next to me on the bed.

"That I was contagious?" I tease.

He laughs, "No, smartass. Because you were pale and clammy. You wouldn't even let me tell you about the checks you asked me to do for you."

That's right. He tried to talk to me yesterday, and it sounded like a jackhammer in my eyeball. That also reminds me of the conversation I had with Franziska yesterday.

It's a worry that the two are linked in my brain. But I

promised her Brian and I would come to dinner. Tonight.

Crap.

First thing's first. I sit up straighter. "You have my attention now, detective."

Through his smile, he says, "Well, it's good news."

"I knew it." I lunge forward, but my body's still not ready for that. White stars circle my head and I lay back before I pass out.

With his hand, he helps guide me back. "Settle petal. I meant good news as in they all came back clear."

How is this good news? I don't get it, but he's looking at me like I should, so I nod.

"Even the FedPol check came back for Lincoln Jones, not even a traffic ticket overseas," he says.

"Well, there you go," I point out. "Who doesn't have a traffic ticket?" Maybe because he rides around in buses all day taking innocent, barely legal adults out with their parents to some loopy loop farm. He doesn't need to drive.

Ah, the tension forms in the back of my neck.

"Babe," Brian continues, "no one is asking you to like his parents, just let them see if they can repair the bond. At least they're trying, you know. Why come back?"

His words are also true and make sense, but it's this feeling inside. I'm off kilter; the world has shifted a degree off its axis. Something is just not right.

Listen to me, I sound like a crazed person.

"So, there was nothing? No charges, no arrests. Nothing. On all of them?" I ask.

Brian nods.

I have no other option. I made a promise. Brian was clear as day, it's me risking his work and his chance to find answers that's haunted him for years. I get his reason and he has asked me specifically to let this go.

So I will.

"Ok." With a heavy sigh, I drop the worries and let the doubt leave. It's already Sunday and Topher will be back tomorrow, anyway.

"Just like that? Ok?" He eyes me suspiciously.

"Well, I made a promise, didn't I?" I say. "Plus, there's something I need to ask you."

"Really?" He sits up straighter and puffs his chest out and takes two deep breaths in. "Go ahead, I'm ready."

I nibble on my fingernail, trying to fight back my smile. "You sure you're finished?"

He fights back his smirk and nods like a living Buddha. I shake my head but still think he is the hottest Buddha I have ever seen.

Reality comes back to me, in the form of a tennis ball in my throat. "So, Franziska rang me yesterday."

His brows crease, I have thrown him off his little performance, but he does well to stay in character.

"She wants me to come up today to see her, but she has asked..." I clear my throat and shuffle in the bed. This is the first time I've invited him to Franziska's house. Who am I kidding? He is the only guy I've invited to Franziska's house, apart from Topher, of course.

He must realise, because both brows raise and the smirk on his face turns into a knowing smile.

"She asked if you want to come to dinner tonight. I said you might work, so you don't have to if you're busy," I blurt and in record time.

Now he has a full-blown smile, and I blush. "I'll make sure I'm there," he answers.

~

Franziska scoops dry black tea leaves, then closes the lid of the clear jar. She opens the green tea leaves, takes a scoop and adds it into the teapot.

"Elita, go to the garden and pick me one red rose petal," she asks as she brews a tea that she says will rejuvenate me.

I felt much better, no longer tired and lacking in energy. But with a bit of makeup, I really thought she wouldn't be able to tell.

What I underestimated is how she always picks up on everything.

"Is a rose petal necessary?" I ask but am already getting up from the kitchen table swiping another puff pastry biscuit that was just freshly baked.

"Yes. Just one and with your left hand." She waves me

off.

"Yeah, yeah, I know." Franziska and her superstitions. I smile, growing up here was never dull.

Standing from the round wooden table, I tuck the chair under so I can open the back door. Franziska has a bit of land size, but the small bluestone cottage off the main street in Tanunda feels like it's getting smaller. Maybe I'm just getting bigger.

I remember the first time she gave me the tour, I could not believe how much stuff she had. My eyes transfixed on glass cabinets, crystals, ornaments, things I had never seen before. That wouldn't have been hard to do since before that mum had us living in a bare bone rented house. It was a maze. So much to explore.

I duck my head through the small path leading me to the back garden. The hanging pots too low for me now.

Even though I couldn't wait to be out of the small town and in the city, there is nothing compared to Franziska's garden nearing the end of spring. I walk through her shade house of undercover plants. The amount she grows and can keep alive is astonishing. She has a green thumb, for sure.

Never once did she have a conventional job. She has always lived off what she sells out of the garden. Whether it be her roses to a select few florists in Adelaide, to strange herbs that are popular in the alternative herb stores, there was a constant flow of customers and work.

And that work kept her busy most of the time. As I grew up, many a day were spent on this very concrete path, walking past the old steel four point hanging line. Walking past the centre garden trough and under a veil of vine leaves. There lies her precious rose garden.

My feet crunch walking on the white gravel that separates the large grouped roses, from the ranges of colours sprouting out from the ground to the crawlers lining the white lattice. I press on with my task, walking to the red roses right in front of me.

With my left hand, I gently lift the petal with my thumb but before I put down my index finger a black angry spider scurries towards me.

I pull my hand back. The sound of the pound in my ears was definitely that of my pounding heart. Tripping over my feet, I stumble backward.

A sharp prick breaks the skin on my bare shoulder just as my back hits the creepers behind me.

"Ouch." I see a small prick of blood that's forming on my finger.

Spiders. I hate spiders. This is the one downside; once I see one, I'm done for. I can feel them creeping up my arm, into the back of my hair. I know there is none on me, but I already make my mind up.

Get the hell out of here.

Quickly, but with my left hand, I snatch off a purple climbing rose from behind me and run back into the house.

As soon as the back door slams shut, I throw the petal out of my hand. Throwing my head down, shaking out my long thick hair.

"Oh my god, do I have any spiders in my hair?" I cry for her to look.

"You and spiders. They are the best things for my plants. You leave them alone." She ignores my irrational panic and swipes the petal from the table.

I flip my head up, taking five long deep breaths in and watch Franziska hold up the pedal. "Purple?" she asks me, confused.

"Take whatever you can get. I am lucky to be out of there alive." My heart rate's slowly getting back to normal.

She cleans it in a bowl of water then sets it in the teapot to brew with the tea I am not looking forward to drinking.

"Why is he not here?" She sets the pot and cups on the table and sits down.

"I told you, he had to work." I take another treat. "He's on early's, so he will be here well before dinner, I hope."

"Not him. Him we will get back to." She shakes her head. "I have something for him, for finishing school."

"Oh." She means Topher. "Didn't I tell you that his parents come back?"

"So what?" She frowns.

I sigh, "They took him to this retreat. Some random wellbeing and holistic something, or whatever. He will be back tomorrow."

"Why would you let him go?" She throws her hands up.

I raise my brows. "What was I meant to do? It's his parents, and he doesn't need my permission."

"You could have thought of something." She shakes her head. "They're no good."

"We don't know that." It's ironic that I'm now defending them. Even as I say the words, I know there is no conviction there. But I made the promise to Brian to let it go.

"Yes, you do. But you don't listen to yourself. Only for survival." She shakes her finger at me. "You don't listen to yourself enough."

"Ha." That gives me a chuckle. "I'm the most stubborn person I know. I listen to myself plenty. Some days I wish my brain would shut up and give me a break."

"Then you will lose your gift."

"Anyway…" I pour the tea first for Franziska but remember at the last minute.

"No other people," she scorns.

"I know, I know. I forgot." I smile. Brian is really going to have a field day here. I was going to give him a heads up, but I opted to add a little fun to the night. Deciding not to tell him about all her random superstitions. Like not pouring the tea from my teapot in others' cup. Why, I don't know. She couldn't explain it to me that made any rational sense. As was a lot of things around here when I was little.

I just went with the flow. Growing up was paradise here, compared to my life before. Who wouldn't like to wake up in their own garden nursery, with an abundance of food and pretty things?

I know I won't like this tea. Never without being forced would I opt to brew a tea over pouring a coffee. The boiling water is cool enough for me to drink without scolding my mouth, and I drink it as quickly as I can without my throat catching on fire.

"Now the purple makes sense," she mutters under her breath.

Eventually I finish and put the cup back on its saucer and shudder.

"Good." she nods and continues, "Now a nice deep sleep and your good to deal with the parents."

I groan but don't argue. No point, she has decided. "Anyway, how was your trip to Adela's?" her sister that lives in Victoria.

She shrugs. "Same. Too many noses in the pie in that family. No good. Now Olivia has been sent to a new school."

"Sent?" I screw up my nose. "She's my age, how can she be sent anywhere? She isn't a kid."

"Don't worry about it. It's their business. She's just testing the waters, she'll come around."

"The last number I have for her was disconnected. Do

you have a new one?" Maybe it's time to check in. Sounds like she's been going through it again. I haven't seen her for a while, not since the last summer of high school when her mother sent her to stay with us for the holidays.

She shakes her head. "I can try to get it for you."

"Yes please, that would be good."

"Now, let's talk about why this boy let you drive here alone."

"What?" My mouth drops open. "Let? Brian does not let my do anything. He doesn't have a damn say in what I do." Well, apart from the not obsessing and investigating this whole Topher thing, but that's different.

"You still no well. Should not be driving."

"You asked me to come here," I throw up my hands, "And I told Brian I was perfectly fine because I was."

"Well, we see when he gets here."

Oh boy, this is probably why I've been single all of my life. I don't even bother to ask Franziska to be nice.

I stand. "When in Barossa, drink wine, I always say." Maybe I drove here, but I can always hitch a ride back with Brian.

~

It so happened that I did not need the wine. After an odd encounter with a candle and hot wax being spilt on Brian, Franziska declared him human. Maybe because he didn't get angry, but after that, it was smooth sailing. As Brian is a charmer, I knew he would have her hooked, too. Ok, now I'm lying to myself. I had a lot of doubt.

Either way, my smile is beaming from ear to ear as somehow, tucked away in my world, my family is getting bigger.

My phone rings in the centre dashboard. I peek down and don't recognise the number. I look at Brian's car in front of me and keep my eyes on the road as I hit the answer button and set it to speaker. He will get mad if I answer calls, I don't blame him, but just in case it's Topher, there is no way I won't answer it.

"Hello?" I answer, my mood still elevated.

A hear a distant cry first then a rushed, "Hello, Elita," in a woman's voice. "I'm sorry I didn't return your call early, I'm swamped here."

Cindy.

I sit straighter and turn the volume up before I turn it back down. The crying, not something I want to hear in stereo. "Cindy, hi." I can hear the crazy house behind her. "Congratulations on the baby."

"Oh thanks, yeah. Super fun times." Her tone does not match the words. But it sounds like her time's short, so I get to the point.

"I know you're busy, so thanks for calling back. I was ringing about Topher and his parents. Do you remember much about the case?"

"Wait, hang on." Her hand must cover the phone, I hear a muffled scream for a Craig to get the kid. I'm guessing Craig must be the doting dad. A door closes, and it's quieter. "Ok. Now where were we? Topher. Case. Yeah, of course I do, everything. You didn't make it one to forget too easily."

"True, but finally we got there, and he could legally live with me."

She laughs. "Till this day, I still don't know how you got me to agree to that. Even though it made the most sense. Anyway, what about it?"

"Well, his parents just came back. They said they were told by the department that he had runaway and was not in the system."

"They said that?" she asks.

"Yeah, to me, then to Topher before he left."

"Where did he go?"

"To this retreat for holistic spiritual wellbeing thing. They took us to a seminar before he left. I don't know, it was weird. But heaps of people were buying it. This whole mindfulness stuff."

"Interesting. But back to the department. No way. That never happened. I had that case open for years after I signed him off. I even remember checking the records two years ago. It just became a habit since I was so nervous about it."

Now I feel bad all over again. I knew she hated lying

for me but it was only six months before he could legally apply for funding to live where he liked. That's what I kept telling myself, anyway. I still feel bad, but forever grateful.

"That's what I thought." It knocks the air out of me. They lied. They one hundred percent lied. But why? Now what do I do?

"Well, just keep your eyes open. I can't tell you any more information about them from the file. But they have the tendencies to be easily led, let's just say."

That was already obvious. "Thank you, Cindy," I say anyway. "I really appreciate you getting back to me. I know this call came out of the blue. You must be so busy."

"Anytime," she says. "Oh, Elita," she calls out before we hang up.

"Yeah?" I answer.

"Don't have kids."

9

The Holistic Knights

MONDAY

I left early for work, leaving Brian in bed and avoiding having to lie to him again. I promised I was going to drop my suspicion of Topher's parents, but after Franziska and the phone call from Cindy, which I decided not to tell him about, it's a promise that's getting harder to keep. Something is off. I just don't know what it is. So until I'm sure, I will keep it to myself.

My desk is on the second level of this small office building just outside of the city, in Norward. The main street on the Parade is out of view but we have a well-maintained reserve for our view. So I can't really complain that I have to walk an extra ten minutes to get a coffee.

Tony isn't in yet, so there's time to do research on Mary, Graham and Lincoln Jones myself.

I start with the usual searches, location, contact details. The system we use is the best, so when there is no fixed address for Mary or Graham, it doesn't sit well. Are they planning on staying? Leaving again? Taking Topher with them? They have a Queensland postal address, possibly because that is where her father was.

I, at least, can find the mobile numbers of Mary and Graham and put them in my phone. Next is Lincoln Jones.

Nothing. No address. No contact numbers. Even being American, how is he not listed anywhere? Not even an Australian business number registered to him.

Maybe it falls under an international business.

My phone rings causing the table to vibrate, looking down I see Topher's name large on the screen.

I snatch it up and answer, "Hey."

"Hey Sunshine," his bubbly voice booms through. I smile until I remember I have to give him the news about his parents lying.

"We leave in a few minutes," I hear a woman's voice call out.

"Yeah, I know." I can hear his footsteps as he replies to the other person.

"Who is that?" I ask.

"Tara," he says. "She's awesome. We met at the workshop and she's coming with us for a quick trip to the Sunshine Coast."

"Wait, what?" I stand from my chair, needing to pace.

"Oh, crap, I forgot to tell you. Mum has gotten us a quick trip up North before we come back for the Holistic Knight Retreat."

"Knight, what?" I shake my head and quicken my pace. "What the hell are you talking about? So, you're not coming back today?"

Shit, now what? Should I tell him now?

"There you are," I recognise Mary's voice.

"Hang on, E," Topher says as the muffled sounds over the phone make me think he is covering the speaker.

I still hear, barely.

"I'm just on the phone to Elita," he says.

"Ok, but after that, you have to give it back," she says.

"Um, yeah, ok," he agrees. "Let me just tell Elita what's going. So she doesn't worry when I don't come home."

Give what back? The phone? No fucking way. She's confiscating his phone, and he is letting her.

"Of course, darling. I can wait," she says.

There is a slight pause. "Oh ok, like literally wait?" Topher laughs as his voice becomes clearer and louder. "Elita, are you there?" He comes back to the phone.

Shit, how am I going to tell him with her standing over his shoulder? I rub the knots in the back of my neck.

Think, Elita.

There is no way I can let him go away. But my hands are tied.

"How long is this Knight retreat for?" I ask as I jump

back on the computer, already searching for it.

A link to the website of Unlocked, the ticket to abundance and wellbeing comes up. I click the link for the upcoming retreat in Coober Pedy, Adelaide.

Coober Pedy the desert? It's in the middle of nowhere, about eight hours away, near the middle of Australia.

"Two weeks," his voice is quieter.

My mouth drops open. Two weeks. Two more weeks listening to this bullshit.

"Did I just hear you won't have your phone? What is that about?"

"Elita," Topher's voice softens and I know the tone, he knows it sounds dumb, so why is he doing it? "It's just part of it. You know, disconnection."

I'm losing him by picking at the teachings; it's time for a different tactic.

"You sound pumped and happy. How has it been?" I ask.

"Oh, my god," the excitement comes back in his voice. "This weekend was great. We did so much meditation. I never knew how important it is, and how great it can make you feel."

I roll my eyes. "That is great." My voice does not match my face, but it doesn't matter, he can't see me. "I'm so jealous. I think I need some of this mindfulness."

"You?" He laughs. "Yeah right, I could never see you here."

"Hey," I raise my tone. "If you can do it, I can do it." Then it hits me. I need to go. I need to go to the retreat.

I hit attend on the website and my mouth drops open. Five thousand dollars a ticket.

Are they insane?

"Well, you didn't seem that interested," Topher says, but it doesn't register as I read through the conditions. Damn, you need a nomination from an already appointed Knight.

"Sorry, what?" I ask.

"You didn't like the first seminar," he says. "I doubt you would be into it."

"It's not for everyone," I hear Mary add in the background. I grit my teeth. I bet Mary is a Knight. That's how Topher can go. She probably fronted the money, too, since Topher doesn't have that much.

"That's not true," I add. I need Mary to get me in there. I will find the money, but I need her to approve my purchase. I need to make that happen. It sounds like meditation was a big part of the weekend, so I use that as my ticket in. "I don't know, I kinda liked the time we all had to close our eyes and sit. It was kinda peaceful." Again, I roll my eyes.

"Really?" he asks.

"Yeah, you know my life. Sometimes it's overwhelming but that twenty minutes..." I pause trying to sell my story, I lower my voice, "It was nice to be still, you know."

I add a hint of vulnerability and push the guilt aside of lying to Topher.

If there was another way, I would do it. But the feeling that he is in danger is screaming at me.

"Oh my god, Elita, if anyone needs this in their life it's you." I frown at that. What is that supposed to mean? "It's so good to forgive the past and give yourself over to the way of holistic abundance."

I clench my fist and bite on my knuckle. This can't be the same computer nerd that left the house only three days ago. When I take my fist from my mouth, I see small indents.

It's time to commit.

"Do you think maybe I can join you?" I ask. "Obviously, I will pay for myself. If you think it will be good for me."

"Oh my god, yes, yes, yes, that would be amazing." He claps. Thank God he's happy about that and still wants me around. Playing along is working.

"Oh, I don't think so," Mary pipes in. I backhand my water bottle on the table, and it flies to the floor. She is going to be a problem. I need Topher on my side.

"Oh, ok." I try to portray my disappointment and sadness, a bit of reverse psychology could do the trick now. "I probably can't be fixed, anyway."

Again, my stomach turns as I know I am manipulating Topher.

"Don't say that," he snaps. "There is nothing wrong with you to fix," he says. "Mum, you said that this retreat will break down the barriers that hold us back from our futures. Elita has done everything to take care of me. She deserves everything Lincoln can give us, too." He takes up my defence.

Come on, Mary, give in. "Look darling, we already had to pull some strings to fast track you to becoming knighted," she says. "I can't see Lincoln saying yes to someone who hasn't attended other training. She will be unprepared for the trials."

Trials? Knighted? How can anyone listen to this conversation with a straight face?

"Topher, it's ok. Don't argue with your mother because of me," I say, hoping Mary can hear me.

"We aren't fighting," Topher says. "I just think it would mean a lot to me if Elita could come and learn, too. She supported me all these years, I think she deserves it, too."

Topher's voice is more earnest than I was prepared to hear. Whatever he thinks is going to happen at this retreat, he really believes it.

"Look," Mary says. "I will be more than happy to vouch for her. I wish we could pay for her but we can't afford that, as well."

"You're the best," he screeches. There are some muffled sounds then he comes back to the phone.

"Did you hear that?" He beams.

My eyes well. "Yeah," I say. She probably thinks I can't afford it, so it's a safe bet I won't come. Little does she know how thrifty I can be. I will find that money.

Either I am right about this and Topher will end up devastated from the betrayal of his parents again, or I will lose him altogether as he follows her on whatever bullshit she has gotten him into.

Either way, I know this ends badly.

"We are coming back on Wednesday and leave Thursday morning. I gotta go now, but I am so excited you're coming."

"Me, too," I say, matching his excitement, whilst inside the realisation hits.

How am I going to explain this to Brian?

~

Before I figure out how to tell Brian, I must tell Tony. I go about this the only way I know. Treats. He loves his sugary pastries, so after a quick run to our local bakery on the Parade, I return and set out the pastries. Just as I pour the coffee, his car parks out front.

Please be in a good mood today.

I grab the report from my early morning debt calls showing the amount that I have already collected, shoving it under my armpit. I opt for the chocolate creamed donut that is his weakness on the small plate, then finish it with the coffee in my other hand.

I stand in his office, ready and waiting. The footsteps sound on the stairs and I prepare myself for a Tony explosion.

He stops in the doorframe; eyes narrowed, his eyes bouncing to all that I am carrying. "What did you do?" he asks.

Really? Why does everyone keep assuming I did something?

"Nothing." I smile, extending the plate to him. "Actually, that's not true." I try to manoeuvre to get the job lists from today. It's difficult considering I have no spare hands.

"Give it to me before you drop it, would ya?" He strides in, taking my offering and continuing to his desk.

"Wait, your coffee, too," I say as I look at his paper laden desk, moving a space from the mess before putting it down.

"Coffee, too?" he scoffs. "You're right, that was the wrong question. What do you want?" he says through his first mouthful of food.

"Well..." I throw down my folder on the desk in front of him, then take a seat in the chair opposite. "I have a favour to ask."

He glances through the papers in the folder, nodding in approval at the amounts I've collected. "Not bad." He sips his coffee. "Better not be another day off to go to some bullshit seminar."

I sink back in my seat.

"You're not buying into that crap, are you?" he booms.

"No way." I shake my head. "But Topher is. He already just went to a weekend retreat, now he's going to some two-week Knight training or spiritual training. I don't know, like cheer camp."

"Sounds fucked up to me. I thought he was smarter than that, with all that computer shit he knows about."

I sigh, "I don't know, this whole thing with his parents coming back and throwing money and trips around, I think it's messed up his head a bit."

"Sounds like a cult to me. You know who you should talk to?" He holds his finger up to me to wait. He rummages through his desk.

My anxiety levels explode as I watch on. "You know I can organise your desk for you?"

"What the fuck for? I know where everything is." A stack of papers drops to the floor and he waves it off. "Here." He picks up a pen and copies a number down from a document. "Jeremy is retired now, we used to work together moons ago, but from my memory he got into all this cult crap. Went deep undercover for some trials. He lives down South, talk to him, see what he can tell you."

"Great." I take the paper. "That is perfect, thanks Tony."

He nods and continues eating his donut as he fires up his computer. I don't move as I haven't even asked him for my favour yet.

"You're still here?" he asks.

"Yep." I nod.

"Fine, take a day off. Go see him," he concedes.

"Um, actually." I bite my lip.

"What? Spit it out, woman."

"I need two weeks off starting from Wednesday."

"WHAT!" He shakes his head. "Two fucking weeks. No. Nope. No way." Eventually his hand lands in the normal position. "Why?"

"Because if I'm going to bring Topher back, I need to go to the retreat."

"Have you lost your mind? You can't go running into a cult, you will end up buck naked, selling flowers on the street and screaming the aliens are coming." He shakes his head. "Then who have I left to work?"

Of course. That is where his concerns are.

"Well, that is exactly my point. I can't let that happen to Topher," I point out.

He rubs his forehead. "He is family, isn't he?"

I nod. "And I have little of it as is."

"Don't you have a hotshot cop as a boyfriend? Tell him to go down and drag his ass back."

Don't I wish it was that simple. I shrug and reply, "He said he checked, and they all came back clear."

"Bloody cops." He shakes his head.

"Hey! Um, hello, I'm with a cop."

"Don't remind me."

I slam my hand on my head, but I can't help the smile on my lips. "When was the last time I had any holidays?" I try a fresh approach.

He screws up his face. After a slight pause, he says, "I don't remember."

I say nothing because he just hit the nail on the head.

"One condition Elita," he starts, but my smile is already plastered on my face. Score one for me. "You are not going until you talk to Jeremy. Understood?" He picks up the paper where he got his number from. "I'm gonna tell him you're going now to see him. He owes me."

"Done and done." I clap. "Thanks, Tony. I swear I will make it up to you. After hours, weekend work. Anything."

"You get the boy back and let him work for me. Then we'll call it even."

Ever since Topher helped him on a case involving hacking an email account, he has been conspiring with Topher to wear me down.

"I don't own him. He can do what he likes, but I will stop pushing him to do what I want him to do. Otherwise, I'm no better than they are."

"Fine, now get out, I got shit to do."

10

The Tech

MONDAY

"No Vehicles Beyond This Point." Bold red letters on the sign hanging from the green iron posted gate, stands between my car and a five-hundred-meter trek to Jeremy's front door. I duck, squinting past the hooded trees draped over the house. There's a gravel driveway, big enough for my car, looks like it even veers off to the back of the house. So why can't I drive to the front door?

Of course, Tony sent me to another nut job. No vehicles? This guy can offer valet parking with the space he has.

"Better not be a waste of time." I slam the gear stick in reverse, easing my foot on the accelerator as I go, not wanting any scratches on the baby from the gravel road. "I can't believe I'm leaving it out here." Deep into Glenalta's hillside, the chances of rocks flying from passing cars elevates my anxiety.

I lock the doors and give my car a quick once over for scratches and approach the gate. With no obvious lock I can see, I give it a push.

I walk the long path to the front door and knock.

The door opens to a tall older man in his late fifties, in good shape, dressed in dark denim jeans with a canary yellow polo shirt. Not what I expected.

"Elita?" he asks.

I nod. "Hi, thanks for taking the time to see me today."

"Come in, Tony says you might have found yourself a cult here in Adelaide?"

I follow Jeremy into the house.

"Maybe, I hope not anyway."

We pass a floor to ceiling library. "What is it you do again?"

"I used to be a PI like you, ended up falling into being a cult expert witness. Now I've spent the last ten years testing and help to make surveillance equipment."

That's when he opens the door to his custom workshop. If Topher could see this place, no way he would leave, let alone be following someone like Lincoln Jones.

"Wow." My fingers run along a small drone.

"Just so you know, that one is forty thousand." He nods at it.

At forty thousand dollars, I back away quick. I don't think I can get Tony to add this to a work insurance claim if I accidentally break it.

Still, the setup is hard to control my itchy fingers wanting to play; I walk to another table with ID card printers, blank cards, magnets and other things I don't even know what they do. I pick up a magnet. What is so interesting about this?

Surveying it, it looks like a magnet you can find at the dollar store. "What does this do?" I show Jeremy.

"You don't have one?" His baffled expression makes me realise just how new I am to this job.

I shake my head.

"You should take it." He walks over and picks up another, turns to the back and shows me a very thin veil of plastic. "What you do," he peels off the plastic, "is stick this close to any lock using a Mag Stripe Card and it will screw up the data on the card and stop anyone able to access whilst the magnet is in place."

"Mag Stripe Card?"

"Hotels, motels, anywhere you see one of these." He shows a card with a magnetic strip on it.

"Like my credit card." That is disturbing.

"No, they use HiCo not LoCo." He must see my confusion as he explains further. "Credit cards need to keep data and predominately does not get recoded. As for hotel room keys, they will get re-written many times a week. If you can get into the room, stick this magnet next to the lock. You can search the place with no one busting in. It doesn't look like a lot, but it is powerful enough to jumble even the most sophisticated LoCo cards."

"Wow." I smile. "I can keep this?" I hold up the magnet.

"Take a few." He nods. "Especially if you are really planning going undercover in a cult. You'll need as much security as you can."

"Thank you," I sigh. "I'm not one hundred percent sure it is a cult yet. What I have seen so far, it isn't religious at all."

"That means nothing." He shrugs. "There are many destructive cults. Let's go sit and talk more."

I take a couple more magnets, shoving them in my back pocket.

"Ah, are these legal?" I ask as I follow him through to the back open plan living area. The windows extend to the entire room, trees towering above us like kids in a treehouse.

"Breaking into hotel rooms is illegal, so just keep that to yourself, yeah?" he says.

Well, isn't that great? Another small little omission I must remember to leave out when talking to Brian.

After Jeremy comes back with coffees he made, he starts with the questions straight away.

"How long has your friend been introduced to this group?" He takes a sip.

"Not long at all. Just a few days, really. It's complicated

because Topher's parents, introduced him to it. He said it's a wellbeing, mindfulness retreat but I went to a seminar myself and it was just..." I shake my head, "Wrong."

"Let me guess, he is maybe early twenties, maybe just finished school. At a crossroads?"

I nod my head. "How did you know?"

"The prey on people in search for something, either the emotionally and financially vulnerable, it's common. Tell me about the parents."

I shrug. "I don't really know them. They left him when he was a teenager with his uncle. From what I looked into myself, they were part of the Fundamentalist Latter-Day Saints Religious group. From there onto what they called a pilgrimage or mission work. And never came back."

"I know that group well, dangerous stuff. They still involved?"

"No. Something must have happened. His mother broke down about how it almost crushed her faith." I bite my lip. "Although there is something about her. I can't put my finger on it, but I bet she lies when she's asleep. That's how good she is at it."

"Well, she has a history of being easily controlled and manipulated, either she thinks whatever she is doing will justify the means at no cost, or she is blindly following her orders of recruitment." He rubs his thumb over his chin. "What else?"

"The seminar was crazy, like a cheer camp. With a tiger

and fire breather. We had to sit for almost twenty minutes thinking about what our lives would look like with holistic abundance with this New Age music and these workers constantly watching us."

"Hypnosis, maybe not full-fledged, but absolutely the beginning of programming," he says.

"Programming?"

"Mind control or undue influence. There are common factors to look for. Thought control is one of them. When used maliciously, they can easily convert meditation to hypnosis. Was anyone talking throughout the time, or over the PA system?"

"The leader. Lincoln Jones. Have you heard of him?"

He takes a moment to think. "No. No, I haven't. But sounds like he is conditioning his followers. Did he use any loaded language, or create his own terminology specific to the group?"

"Yeah, I guess." I look up, remembering. "Tickets, we all have tickets from our past that need to be ripped up. He got people up there and completely annihilated them, really diving into personal things. Even with Topher. He and his mother were up on stage, and there was so much pressure for Topher to forgive her. It was hard to watch."

"What he was also using there is emotional control, manipulating people's emotions and response to push the narrative of the group. So, it adopts the group's doctrine as truth. Having a breakthrough, on stage in front of people, will distort the reality of the emotional highs and lows a person feels. It's also called love-bombing."

"He was on such a high after." My stomach is churning with dread.

"So he already has been to this weekend retreat?" he asks warily.

I swallow and nod. "Why, is that bad?"

"It's not great." His honesty knocks me around. "It only takes a few days to establish thought control. Next step is usually a two-week retreat. Then you might not see the person for years. Two weeks is all it takes. You can go from your average person to being under mind control of the leader."

"That's where he's going this week." I sit up. "A two week Holistic Knight Retreat."

"You can't let that happen."

"I know, but I have no choice. That's why I'm here. I should be able to score a ticket to the trip."

"Then you need to be prepared. If your friend has already spent that much time with him..." He shakes his head.

"That's not true. It isn't too late. I know if I find some dirt on Lincoln Jones that proves he is a piece of shit, Topher will listen to me."

"If you go undercover in the cult, you need to prepare for him to turn on you."

I shake my head fervently. "No, he won't."

"Then you are severely under-prepared for this,"

I sigh. "What can I do? How do I prepare?"

"Well, that is why you're here," he says. "Let's get to work, we need an entry and exit point, set up outside communications because no doubt they are controlling the information you can receive on the trip. And you need to get ready to eat a lot of shit and take a lot of shit because they will try to control your behaviour, where you sleep, eat, and your body."

I rub my neck, kneading the knots forming.

"And believe me, once you're on day three of no sleep, deprivation of food and constant indoctrination session, even the best of us struggle to not get affected. He's also practising hypnosis, that there is where you really need to be careful."

"I just won't do it."

"Then you will be cast aside and ostracised, it won't help your cause. You need to sustain day long sessions of meditation and chanting without being programmed."

"How did you do it?"

He shakes his head. "That's something I don't tell anyone. No matter who you are, it's the only thing that keeps me safe. You just need to find a way that you can drown out the outside influence during those sessions."

"Like headphones or music?"

"I don't see how you could hide that, but along the lines." I chew on my thumb, trying to think of something.

"Where is the retreat?" Jeremy asks.

"Coober Pedy."

"Excellent, I have contacts there. I can get you a ride out if you need. We'll set it up."

I nod.

"Alright." He stands. "Come on. We have a lot of work to get you ready."

That's an understatement. I won't lie and say I'm not scared that I might end up on the street selling flowers like Tony said. But I won't let that happen, I need to get Topher back.

I follow Jeremy into the workshop. I'm not out of there until well after three a.m.

11

The Goodbye

TUESDAY

This is the third time he circles the car. The breeze from the water tapers my simmering rage. I push off the alley wall between the Fisherman's Market and my warehouse.

"So?" I swallow hard. "What do you think?" He's had enough time.

"I will give you seven for it." He stops in front of me.

This is why I hate people. The price is the same I paid only three months ago. "It's listed for ten." I might only need five thousand to get a ticket, but the car is worth way more than that. My car. The one that I set out to buy, saved, scrimped and bled for.

"Look..." He takes out an envelope. "Honestly, I have eight thousand dollars of cash only." He shows me the green notes. "Take it or leave it."

I wish I had more time to sell the car. Then, I'd tell him to shove his money. Or better yet, just throw the money in the air and say no deal. But he's the first to reply to the ad I placed this morning. And eight thousand is enough to get the ticket and another car.

"Fine." I snatch the envelope. "Deal." I pull out the papers to get this done. He tries to start a conversation, even tries to hit on me. He soon absorbs the disdain directed his way and stops talking altogether. The rest of the exchange is quick and sharp. Just like a stab wound to the heart.

I don't just see the irony, but I watch it being driven down the street, tyres screeching around the corner until it's gone.

The first thing I do when inside is pour a stiff drink. There's a knock at the door. Is it wishful thinking hoping the buyer is back, wanting to hand back my car? The knocking continues in a familiar pattern only Brian does. Talk about timing. Luckily he wasn't here ten minutes earlier. There's a lot I haven't filled him in on. Starting with me selling my car to finance a trip to a Holistic Knight Retreat. Actually, I haven't even told him about the retreat at all. We keep missing each other and he has been very busy chasing the promotion he needs.

None of that is something I want to do, so I take the drink with me to the door. Sipping, I open it.

"Hey." Brian's there, hand resting on the door frame.

I open the door wider. "Howdy, partner." I lean forward greeting him with a kiss then backing away to let him in.

"Good, you're starting early." He nods to my drink. "That's why I'm here to grab you. We're all meeting at Joe's for some drinks." He nods to the idling car with his partner Max waiting. He sees me and waves. I wave with my drink hand and he beeps for me to hurry.

This got even worse.

"Brian, I don't think I can tonight, I have heaps of work to do." I turn back to him. How the hell am I meant to tell him about the trip? I stall a little longer. "Anyway, is there a special occasion for these drinks or is it because it's a day that ends in Y?"

This has him smiling again, the dimple saying hello. "Not that special, but definitely the last one for a bit. They put us on a task force for a few weeks. Gonna be very intense and time orientated."

"Oh, that sounds all types of interesting, what's the chances you can fill me in?"

"None and fuckall." I laugh and he pulls me in closer. "Just sucks, I won't have much free time for a few weeks."

"This is big for your promotion, right?" I ask.

He nods.

"I will come find you guys after I'm done with work." I give him a quick kiss before he leaves. "This is good news. And don't feel bad, because I haven't told you yet. I'm going on a two-week retreat to Coober Pedy tomorrow."

"You're what?" His eyes go wide.

"Um, yeah. Long story, but it was a spur-of-the-moment decision."

"And what, you couldn't text?" He sounds pissed.

I scrunch my nose. Good point, why didn't I? Oh, that's right, because I was lying to him and specifically went against our promise. "I'm sorry, I just thought I'd talk to you tonight. It was just so sudden." That's an understatement.

"Wait," his eyes narrow and I swallow hard. "You just go on a two-week trip without a heads up?"

"You're going to be busy anyway, so what's the big deal?"

"You didn't know that."

"Obviously, I'm not psychic." This is ridiculous. Or maybe it's me, I'm so new to this relationship stuff, but I know it's the lying that's coming between us and that's my fault. I need to fix it.

"I'm sorry, you're right," I say. He doesn't hide his disappointment. I'm the world's worst girlfriend. It's hard to remember that for some reason I have to report my whereabouts and goings on to another person. "We can talk about this tonight; Max is in the car waiting."

He turns to the car. "Max, give me ten minutes," he calls out, then walks past me and into the kitchen. I sigh and down the rest of the drink and cheers it to Max. He is shaking his head and laughing. I guess everyone knows about me at the station.

I don't realise it's oddly quiet until I see Brian leaned over casually looking at the coffee table. The table I had been doing research on, with all my files laid out all over it. Crap, I completely forgot about that.

Why didn't I think of that first before this stupid drink?

"This is you dropping it?" There is no excuse for the stacks of information Jeremy had me read before I go. The files I created on my own for Lincoln Jones, Mary and Graham. He points to the criminal checks I ran myself. "You know I already gave you the all clear."

"I know. They aren't like what you could do, though. Plus, I had done them earlier."

"Right, so guess I won't be making detective anytime soon?" He shrugs.

"Um, why is that?" I furrow my brow.

"Because apparently even my girlfriend thinks I'm shit at it."

That is a hop, skip and a jump over dramatic. "Brian, that is not what I think at all. Why would you say that?"

"Your actions show different."

"And your actions show that I have to hide my concerns rather than come to you about them. Is that true, too?"

"Of course not, you know that." He runs his hands through his hair.

I really don't want to fight. "Look, there is only a problem if we make it a problem. I just wanted to be prepared."

"Prepared for what?" He looks down at some papers. "Destructive Mind Control?" He shakes his head, reading the title of one paper on the table. "You can't see it, can you?"

His soft eyes find mine, and I don't see anger or disappointment anymore. "Your obsession is clouding your judgement."

It takes a while for the words to sink in.

"I don't mean to sound like a dick, babe, and I want you to know I say it because I love you." He lifts my chin from looking to the ground and back to his. "I think it will be good, maybe it's just what you need."

He leans his forehead on mine. "I'm sorry, too. You can always come to me, ok?" He leans in and gives me a kiss. "Come meet us after."

And this is the first time I don't really want to.

~

After the terrible fight with Brian, the rest of the day is filled with preparation. Organising the tickets, shopping for the trip and having to get the authorisation from Mary for acceptance. Although, hearing the surprise in her voice when I said I had the money was almost worth selling my car. Almost.

I looked long and hard for another option, but if I want to check-in at the motel room before two to set up my equipment, I need to be on the last bus out at eleven that night. There's no other choice. I vow to still make it to drinks tonight for Brian.

I fly upstairs, throwing the suitcase Jeremy had given me on the bed. The black, plain bag disguises the bottom secret compartment. I throw in the protein bars, water and sugary sweets. In case food is not easily accessible. Jeremy is right, being deprived of necessities is a scary notion. It would be for me, but it was a staple from my early childhood. Still, I need to make sure I am mentally sharp. I mark that off the checklist.

I open my usual suitcase that I will leave at the motel room and shove some bubble wrap in the bottom to pack the tech. My 'just in case' bag. The recorder for the bug, research, notes, laptop. My wig and hat for a disguise if needed. What else? I whiz around thinking of things I could need.

I grab the paper and check the list, most already done. The one that keeps gnawing at me is how to avoid being hypnotised through meditation. What would be the point of me going to protect Topher if I'm brainwashed alongside with him?

What is something that's going to keep that from happening? Jeremy says that headphones won't work, but how am I meant to block out his voice if it's anything like what happened at the seminar?

I need a distraction, something that will take my attention away from falling under a spell. But covert enough, it won't draw attention to me.

That's it.

I sprint to the small linen cupboard we packed full of unboxed items from our move. One after the other, I search until I'm left with the small microchip. Bingo. I have no idea how it works, but the Annoy-A-Tron might just be the thing to save me.

It's small enough I can put somewhere in my clothes along with the magnets I have to carry. If I need to, I can turn it on, and it's an instant distraction. Perfect.

After that, the packing goes quick. All my clothes designed to have some area to store the devices undetected. Enough calories and water to keep my energy levels sustained and all my other tools I can store at the motel.

For the first time since I started, I check the time. Only two hours before the bus leaves. By the time I get to Brian, I will only have twenty minutes tops before I have to get to the bus. I dial the number for the cab and trek my bags down while I order my ride.

Cash goes a long way. I hand the driver a fifty to wait, promising I won't be long, and run into Joe's, a small bar that most of the precinct drink at. A quick scan and I see a small group that work with Brian at the station in the corner. But not Brian.

I walk towards the bar, the only other logical spot he could be. Once I get through a small crowd playing pool, I spot him leaning on the bar talking to a petite blonde woman. She throws her head back and laughs, reaching for her beer and taking a drink.

I don't break stride as I approach. "Hey." I come up to Brian's side.

"Elita." Brian looks at me shocked. "You made it."

"I told you I would." I really don't want to fight, not when I have so much going on. Finally, I found someone that I love and can trust. I won't let an argument or my own issues get in the way.

Even if he is sitting here talking to some hot chick.

"Oh wow, you're Elita?" The blonde beams. "You're infamous at the station."

I blow out a breath. "It's all not true, I'm not that bad." I'm realising cops are more gossipy than high schoolers.

"Oh, uh, Liz is the new station clerk," he introduces. "Liz, this is Elita."

"Finally, I get to put a name to the face." She looks me up and down. "Interesting," she mutters.

Disregarding her snide comment, I turn to Brian. "Can I talk to you for a minute?" I nod for some privacy. "I can't stay for long."

His mood changes, but I already know how I'm going to fix it.

"C'mon." I grab his hand, pulling him up from the bar.

He drags his feet but follows. "Babe, I'm not looking for round two," he says as I finally find the right door.

I recall the utility room on my last trip to the bathroom at the bar. I remember because I was red hot and ready to go that night, but Brian was in a tournament at the tables.

This time I shove him in and close the door.

"I don't want to fight, either." I push him against the door to stop anyone from entering and my lips land on his. "We have ten minutes to say goodbye," I get out between kisses.

His hands waste no time in taking over, sliding under my ass then turning me so I slam back into the door. With his strong arms holding me up, I use both my hands to take off my top.

"Fuck me," he growls.

"Well, duh, that's the point!"

And we use the last ten minutes together to say our goodbyes. A connection we both desperately needed after being so far apart. I succumb to the passion between us, the connection that became too strong to avoid the emotional feelings that bombarded me.

Love.

This is why I'm here, making things right with Brian. After we're dressed, he walks me out the front to the waiting cab.

"I'm going to miss you." He pulls me in for one final kiss.

"Me, too." No point anymore denying it. "At least you will be able to one hundred percent concentrate on this job. I know how important it is to you."

"It is."

"Just remember to keep checking your phone. I don't know if I'll be allowed to keep mine, but you know I will find a way to contact you," I say.

"If anyone can, you can," he chuckles. "Have fun and try to enjoy yourself, ok?"

His warm, green, genuine eyes stare at me with love and worry. He still thinks I'm over-reacting and thinks that I'm taking a trip for a vacation.

I decide to give him that. No point for him to stress about me. "You're right, I think it will be good for me. Maybe get me in the holiday mood for when you finish your case. We could do a little R&R trip ourselves."

His eyes light up. "Done!"

With our future set, we say goodbye with a long, sweet kiss before the cab door slams closed and I drive away.

Before I do, I unwind the window and call out, "you can go back to flirting with Bitchy Better now."

He throws his head back and laughs as the cab pulls into traffic and I wave my goodbye to Brian.

12

The Retreat

WEDNESDAY

There's not much to this cheap motel. It's clean, that's good, and close to the hotel we have to meet at to catch the bus to the retreat. It's a two-minute walk and from there we board on two buses. After a fifteen minute drive, we should arrive at the underground campsite.

So, by my calculations, it's over an hour on foot. Further than what I had hoped for, but still doable if I need to get back here. It makes little sense to leave my phone, if I need it in a hurry then I will need it close.

I have to take it with me but if they confiscate it, I'm screwed. With my burner phone in one hand, my smartphone in the other, the only option is to swap the sim cards. In case Jeremy is right and Topher sees, I don't have the same handset. My stomach twists from thinking this way. But if I want to stay objective, I have to think of all options. Packing away my burner phone with my contacts on it in the suitcase, my first job when I get there is to find a safe place to stash it.

Leaving my gear at the hotel, I take only what I need, and walk down the long road to the hotel.

I see a crowd forming in the horizon with two large charter buses. Topher must be there, so I walk faster. Losing breath, I reach the group and perch my head higher to look above the bodies. My feet on tiptoes, I finally spot his head walking behind Lincoln Jones and his parents talking to some younger looking Smurfs.

He looks normal, that's a good sign. I make my way towards him when a bright eyed, bouncy redhead stops in front of me.

"Howdy, name hunny?" She has her pen ready to write it on the form.

"Um, Elita." I look to her but don't want to miss my opportunity of talking to Topher.

"Yep." She finally finds my name. "You're on this bus." She points to the one closest to me. My bags are lifted from my hand by a Smurf popping gum, this one with brown hair and looks about my age. He smiles as he wistfully collects all the luggage from the guests.

"Ok great, I just needed to–" I point towards where Topher is.

She laughs, "Yes, yes, we all want to talk to him, Lincoln will have time for everyone, don't worry."

I force myself to make sure my face does not move. It's hard fighting against how wrong that statement is, with not even just an eye roll.

"I mean, I see a friend, not Lincoln. I wanted to catch up with him first."

"Who?" she asks.

"Topher, do you know him?" I ask.

"Oh yeah, that's Mary and Graham's son. Oh wait, you're the one we got through last night." She holds up her hand. "Sarah," she calls out over my head.

When I turn, I see her. I don't even have to know I'm right to know the blonde hair, thin woman jumping up and down in a flowered sundress is Sarah.

"Sarah is going to be your buddy. This is her first time here, too." I don't believe that for a second, but I wave. Jeremy had said there were jobs given to watch over people. Sarah is my handler and that fake smile she has planted on her face, while she dodges and weaves her way through the crowd to get to me, I don't buy for a second.

"Is this her?" Sarah barrels toward me, throwing her arms around me in a hug, a complete disregard for my personal space.

I pat her gently three times before pulling away. "I'm Elita, I think we're buddies." There's no point in getting off to a bad start.

"I'm so excited! Can't you feel it in the air? Are you

ready for what's about to happen?" With both her hands, she squeezes my arms, peering deep in my eyes. Sarah is a tad intense.

I nod slowly, but they lose my attention when I see one bus pulling out. I scan the crowd and Topher is no longer there. Dammit, he's gone.

Sarah grabs my hand and leads us to board the bus on our way to the retreat. She chatters constantly, introducing me to everyone, sharing the high spirits. My head hurts from all the nodding, my jaw from all the smiling and my brain from all the time I had to refrain myself about the nonsense they sprout.

Everyone is running through what they know about the teachings. Some even have notebooks already half-filled. Some even have multiple notebooks bragging about all the tickets they have already torn up, and how Lincoln has changed their lives.

I can see how easy it can be to get caught up in the positive vibes. The messages are easy to believe, and who wouldn't want to be their better selves? I'm not sure why they need this guy to tell them to get over their shit and move the fuck on from their past, I could tell them that for a lot less than the five thousand dollars.

I zone out from the noise of the group and I pay attention to the surroundings and the direction we're going. The trees are sparse and very few between. I hope there are some places around the campsite so I can hide my phone, maybe in the branches, or there could be a rock. I must find something.

We pull into the carpark and I'm glad it's not a complicated track back. I should be ok without having to stick to the main road. If I have to, I can make it to the motel with no problems.

The bus pulls to a stop and we pile out, the excitement still buzzing in the air. There's a line forming and we follow suit and take our place.

"Wait, what about our bags?" I turn to go back to the bus.

"It's ok." Sarah grabs my hand to stop me. "They will take it to our rooms they said."

Crap, I really hope this isn't their way of going through our stuff. I know it's a secret compartment, but my bag is on the heavy side. This is not a good start.

"Everyone follow me," the redhead says.

The air is thick and hot, it's not summer in Adelaide but we are so far into South Australia the sun pummelling down feels like it is. The sweat is beading up the back of my neck. I scan for the closest air conditioning and see only one large building, more like a tin shed, desolate and sad, with no sign of any cool air.

We are all huddled into a line, Sarah in front of me. She turns and winks. "Here we go!"

A bin sits on the table for us to put our belongings in. Mindlessly we all do as we're told and drop our phone, or in my case fake phone, into it.

Once we get to the front of the line, Lincoln Jones stands at the entrance, right beside a large antique wooden box. He stands, chest puffed and on a pillar. He calls next. I watch as Sarah walks regally forward. She bows her head. I can't make out what he says. Then she hands him something. I'm looking hard but I can't see anything, but whatever it is he puts it in the chest.

He waves her off and calls next again.

My turn.

I walk towards Lincoln Jones; I stop in Sarah's footsteps, focused on not being any different to a real believer.

"I am your God," Lincoln Jones says. His eyes pin me down, commanding obedience.

I stand stunned.

"Give me your voice," he continues. "If you talk, I shall kill you. If I deem fit, I shall kill you, I am God." He opens his hands out for me to hand him something.

This is the first few minutes and already I'm proven right. This guy is bat shit crazy and I can't believe for one second Topher willingly fell for this shit. My eyes shift behind him to see if I can see Topher in the crowd of voiceless people that are milling around in the middle of the campsite.

I don't see him and I have no more time; I do as he says. With both hands, I reach for my voice and hand it to Lincoln Jones, his eyes never leaving me, watching.

His dominance on the pillar, looking down at me is intimidating. He places my voice in the box with the rest of people's right to object and ask questions.

He is smart, this solves the problem of people voicing their concerns. Me voicing my concerns.

"Next!" He dismisses me.

I scurry out of the line; I dodge Sarah as I hide, following behind two older women. When I see the guy in a blue shirt with bags, one of them mine, I follow.

I stalk through the crowd and keep a firm eye to where he goes. I do this until he disappears into a caved entrance inside a large opening of a mine site.

Arms wrap around my waist from behind and I jump. I am turned quickly and see Topher's glowing face. I open my mouth to talk, but his finger flies to his lips to warn me of it.

I throw my arms around him and give him a hug. He squeezes me back. He motions and waves his hands around, looking amazed.

I give him a thumbs up.

I throw my hands up, trying to ask where he has been? He screws up his face, trying to understand. I mouth, "How are you?"

His eyes go wide and looks around. Once he sees no one is paying attention, he turns back to me and zips his lips with his fingers.

This time I roll my eyes and hear the familiar laugh.

At this, I smile and mouth, "Missed you."

He answers with another hug.

Huddled in the centre, red dirt beneath us and the penetrating sun above, Lincoln Jones steps onto a pedestal.

What is with him and his pedestals?

"Today marks the beginning of your transformation. Follow all, without question, without hesitation, and by the time you walk out of here, I will ascend you into a life with an unfathomable amount of abundance in all aspects of your being. You will truly be a Holistic Knight."

The applause sounds, the excitement overwhelming one of the women from my bus calls out a, "Whoo hoo!"

"You!" His finger points directly at her, his voice deep and powerful, changing the mood instantly. "Die."

There are a few gasps at his words. My mouth drops open when she falls flat on the floor. Our heads swing back to Lincoln Jones, who stands above the sun shining down on him.

This is absurd. I peek around, and it looks like I'm the only one that thinks it. Eyes glued open, mouths shut.

I look back when he continues to talk, "Everything is connected. Everything has a meaning. Do you think this place so remote and derelict is somewhere I would choose for a retreat? A retreat so meaningful, so trans-formative just because of convenience?"

He rubs his hands together, a real showman, reaching out and opening it up. A Smurf, or as he calls it Spirit Crew, puts something in his hand. This time not make believe.

"This is an opal and there is an opal mine." He points to another large rock formation on the opposite side. "Opal will strengthen your cosmic consciousness and enhance your mystical and physical visions. And you all will sleep surrounded in it."

"Follow me now, into the workroom." He motions to the tin building. "Let the trials begin."

~

The workshop is hours long, competitive tasks, racing sacks, and trust games. The rule is if God, AKA Lincoln, says you die, you have to drop dead there and then. Bodies lay everywhere. Hours have passed. The sun is setting out of the small window of the tin shed.

Once the sun sets, it gets cold, and for the people on the ground they stay there. I realise this when we are walking back down a path towards the main building. Thankfully Lincoln already announced we were about to have dinner.

But there are people still pretending to be dead. Isn't the game over? Lincoln leads the way and makes no move to stop. He's going to have dinner and let them go. How long is this meant to last for?

I know I should get as much substance as possible, but while we roamed the campsite in silence with only

Lincoln's voice preaching his bullshit, I found the perfect spot for my phone and if I want to plant it there, this is the perfect time.

I know where all the bodies lie, and where everyone will be for at least a half an hour for dinner.

If I die right where I am now, I will have a clear view of the dining hall, and back access to the cave entrance. No one will see me get my phone.

"I'm so glad we get to eat now," I say out loud.

Everyone stops walking. Lincoln Jones stops walking, instead of his usual point and die routine, he strides towards me.

I feel Topher's eyes on me.

He stops one foot from my face. It's then I realise why he carries the pedestal with him. He is much shorter than I even expected. Regardless of his height, he dominates the area he is in with his confidence and arrogance.

His eyes sweep up and down, slowly and not trying to hide his disappointment. He shakes his head. "You are weak. Die."

Against my natural response from wanting to kick him in the balls at that comment, I drop to the floor. He turns, his shoe kicking dirt in my face, grains get in my already dry and brittle mouth.

I watch with hatred in my eyes as he leads the dozen that are still alive into the dining hall. As soon as the door closes, I do a quick scan.

All clear.

I jump up and run back through the way we came, coming up to the back way to the entrance of the cave. The entrance is a sitting area, very basic but comfortable. There are three ways I can go. Left, right, and down?

He said we were sleeping surrounded by opals, so I go forward down the dark steps. There is a light glow leading through caved walls, the carvings intricate and unique on the tunneled walls. I find a large flat area, bags and luggage sprawled out.

With no time to waste, I run and search. But can't find my bag. There are curtains surrounding the space. I run to one and rip it open. Bunks are stacked up into a small enclave.

If I weren't well versed in hiding from my childhood, I might hate the thought of such confined spaces. He must have a reason for putting people in this tiny room.

My bag is not there. I run to the next space and the next. As it goes, the last enclave is where I find it. I make quick work of getting it out, not even stopping for some food or water. I still need to plant the phone and get back in case anyone notices.

My heart pounds the entire time, but I make it back to my death spot after a successful mission. Laying my head on the ground for a split second, a wave of dizziness hits. Maybe I should have had some of that water.

I close my eyes for a second and take a moment to rest

and control my heart rate.

I don't know how long passes when I hear his voice.

"All up and come gather," Lincoln Jones announces with a megaphone. He calls out over and over as bodies slowly rise. Some have been laying in the same spot for over six hours, even longer. They are helped by a couple of Smurfs.

Once we gather, he turns to Topher and four others. They stand waiting, smiling. Proud of their accomplishment at surviving.

"Your arrogance and need to outsmart the game has you failing in life," he announces to a stunned Topher, who slumps his shoulders. I clench my teeth to stop from showing emotion.

"You need to die before you are reborn. You need to die before you can ascend. But you want to hold on to the past so much, you want to be valued so much you miss the basic comprehension of this lesson.

"In front of you on the floor is a gun." I push forward to the front, having to check. A deep, long breath escapes when I see he is talking about pretend things again.

"Pick it up." He points to the ground.

I can't look away, I watch transfixed as all five of them pick up the imaginary gun.

"Open your mouth and put it in there," his voice now in the background of my mind. My face falls when I see Topher blindly follow.

"Now kill yourself. For me."

Like flies, they drop to the floor, all five of them pulling the imaginary trigger.

I feel a tear fall at the terrifying sight.

13
—

The Belladonna

THURSDAY

It is well into the middle of the night when I ate a few bars and drank some water. Everyone else sleeping in either a bunk or a small tent.

It only felt like a few hours before they woke and ushered us to the dining area for breakfast. Still no one speaks, unsure if they'll allow us. Or maybe because we're already exhausted, starved and dehydrated. I don't even think half the people here had anything to eat at all yesterday.

When I enter the small space, the room fills with voices. That answers one question. I flop in the first free seat, Sarah across from me staring into space, eyes locked on the table in front of her.

She looks up at my movement. "Do you think I'm vain?" she asks.

"I don't really know you." I shrug and her shoulders slump. "Why are you asking?"

"I lost a ring that has been in my family for a long time last night. Lincoln says it's a reminder of what was tying me down and to not keep looking for it. That my vanity makes me want to hold on to it. I have spent all night journaling, and I think he might be right."

"Maybe, but I guess it isn't really yours to lose. Even if you don't wear it, you might regret not finding it if you can."

"And go against what he said?" She leans back in her chair, sitting taller. She shakes her head.

"Ok, up to you." I shrug. I'm not capable of fixing her problems, nor in the position to.

"You're right. Please come with me. Can you help me look for it? I don't think I can do this alone, I might not be able to."

She won't be able to find it herself, or go through with going against what Lincoln says? Either way, I don't want to do it, either. I look past her to the food and my stomach rumbles.

"Please, Elita. You're my buddy, I have no one else to ask."

Fuck.

I push my hands up on the table getting out of the chair. "Let's hurry, I'm starving."

She doesn't waste any time and we back track her

steps to where she died, not too far from the crime scene was her ring. She hugs me excessively before I remind her that food is waiting.

But as we approach, the door to the dining room is closed by a Smurf, and our group is forming two lines back onto the bus.

I look back to Sarah. "I'm sorry," she winces. "Maybe we're going into town."

I suck in my anger and find my place in line, saying goodbye to the much needed breakfast I missed.

~

The black figure is walking closer. It's hard to tell if this finally is another person. I try one more time to find some saliva to wet my cracked lips, my water ran out what feels like an hour ago.

I run now, away from the looming arms. It's not real. This is not real.

Dropping to my knees, I run the dirt between my fingers. The ground brings me back to where I am. I shake my head until I remember.

I sit flat on my bum, sweat dripping down my face. They dropped us all in the desert to camp under the stars. He said there would be nothing stopping us from connecting ourselves with Mother Nature herself. Now I find myself closer than I have ever been to nature.

And I hate it.

Breakfast feels like days ago, and I don't remember seeing anyone for such a long time. I'm left here alone with my tent and my thoughts. Thoughts that have me racing around this desolate space to escape.

This can't be real. What is happening? They had given us only one bottle of water. I sipped slowly, not wanting to drink too fast. Now I'm wondering if there was something in it. Or is this really because of the environment he has willingly put us in? Either way, this is so dangerous that he will not get away with it.

I drag my arms and legs through the sand until I find the tent I left behind. With my hands, I push myself up. When I stretch back to my full height, my mother stands in front of me.

I jump back, tripping over a small rock. My ankle lands off balance, but when I look back to where I saw her, she's gone. Still trying to back away, my foot slips down a hole. An open mining shaft more like it.

As the weight pushes me backwards, I fall deeper in the hole. Desperate not to fall, I cling to the rocks above. My knees scrape as I stop myself from falling inside an open mining site. With most of my body still above land, I use what I have left in my strength to pull myself up. But I freeze at the sight in front of me.

A flower begins to sprout from nowhere. Magically growing into gorgeous pinkish petals. I recognise it instantly.

A belladonna lily.

I know this plant. Franziska used to sell it before one day she ripped it from her plantation. She said that it can put people to sleep; she called it the sleeping beauty of all her plants. Only a pinch, not much, and you will have a slumber like no other. But something happened back then, and now they're were all gone.

Once I'm up, I pluck it from its roots. I don't ask question; I don't even think it's real. I take the plant and sprint forward to my tent, eyes in front looking for the warnings signs I missed earlier.

Back in the tent, I zip it shut, hiding again. I rock back and forth, shaking the black memories I have stored away. Hiding away while she's out there. My mother. The people she had over. Just hiding.

It's just a hallucination, I tell myself repeatedly, but it doesn't help. My body convulses petrified she will find me. They will find me. I really do not want to be here anymore. My eyes water, I feel the tears. The diary they left in the tent laughing, taunting me.

Write my fears.

Write my weakness.

Write, write, write.

That was drilled in over and over on the bus on the ride over. No. This is not real.

Just like all he says, it isn't real. It is not that easy to tear apart your tickets.

A loud cry comes from deep inside me. What is happening to me? The tent is closing in, my chest is rising and falling too fast.

I lay down, curled until a black figure with long hair is waiting outside my tent. I slam my eyes shut, rocking and chanting it isn't real.

Until finally I fall asleep.

~

The water stings my body. They only provided us with a small amount of sunscreen on our camping trip in the blazing heat. How much I had been craving this shower crushed as soon as the water hit my red skin.

I waited until everyone had used the facilities, so grateful they even had running water.

Something happened out there, maybe the dehydration or lack of food and sleep. Or a drug in the water. Whatever it was, it has taken its toll. I don't think I can do this for two weeks. There is no rest or downtime. I still haven't been able to even get close enough to Topher to even talk, let alone privately. It can't be a coincidence we are always being separated.

My body is crumbling, and it's getting weak. Jeremy told me this was going to happen, he said I wasn't prepared. So arrogantly I told him I would be fine. Maybe I thought he was overreacting. Are all these people crazy or am I? Why am I the only one who sees how dangerous it is, how clearly delusional, sickening and twisted?

Topher put an imaginary gun in his mouth and blew his brains out. That image will screw with my head for a long time. I try one of Jeremy's tricks, turning the hot water faucet off. My body tenses as freezing water pummels down. He says it's a way to rejuvenate my cells and bring my brain back into focus. I need my mind right again before I go back out. I don't know what's in store for me.

Turning off the water, I get dressed, making sure I've got my devices and everything hidden away. It's a small shower allotment; about seven cubicles. I waited until I was the last one, to have the place to myself. I hear a commotion outside. I decide to leave my hair wet just in case we're in for another hot day outside.

To my surprise, the crowd is walking to the dining hall. This time no one is going to stop me. I'm going to find Topher. And eat.

When I walk in, I notice straight away everyone has a red complexion. The mood is relaxed or just too tired to even talk. I spot Topher sitting in the back corner with the same group from the hotel.

The last time I was in this room, I failed to eat anything. I'd stand in line to the food buffet first. As I wait, I watch everyone standing quietly, some whispering and talking. Lincoln Jones is nowhere to be, just high-ranking

Smurfs. Something feels off.

When I pile the food on my plate, I can feel my tummy already rejecting it. But I want to see if I can get as much substance in as I can. I've been lucky enough to have snacks in my luggage. If I weren't afraid of sharing and getting caught, I would. Some of these people clearly look like they're struggling.

When I reach Topher's table I don't ask, I just take a chair and sit across from him.

He breaks conversation from one girl he was talking to and focuses his attention on me.

"Hey." I realise I'm not sure what to say. This is new. Me having to censor myself around him. I should have thought about this before I approached.

"How amazing was yesterday?" He leans forward.

"That is definitely one way to put it." He doesn't get angry, he just laughs, more relaxed.

"On our trip yesterday, I can't believe how much of a breakthrough I had. You would be so proud of me." He sounds like them.

The girl next to him bumps him. "So, are you going to introduce us?"

I take a bite of the potatoes, Topher looks between the two of us nervously. "Elita, this is Kelly..." he pauses. "My girlfriend."

The now mashed potatoes fly out of my mouth and splutter all over his face. I was nowhere near prepared to hear those words ever come from his mouth.

"That is disgusting." He wipes his face with a napkin.

"You're what?" My voice is louder than I mean it to be since I'm unable to control my shock.

He leans in closer. "Shh!" He looks around to see if anyone is looking. "You're just sounding like a blocker. I've made so many breakthroughs that I didn't even realise when I was limiting my beliefs."

"Being gay is not limiting at all." I can't believe what I'm hearing. He truly has changed. And it's not his fault. My mind can hardly make educated decisions after only a few days here. I went from being starving when I walked in here, to having now lost my appetite.

"I know that," he says, "but if I don't test and figure out what my limiting beliefs are, then how will I know I didn't choose to do something just to punish my religious parents who abandoned me? Maybe you're my form of punishment to them."

"You're putting a lot of emphasis on things that did not matter to you only a few weeks ago." He leans in closer and so does his girlfriend. It's like there are ears everywhere. I want to have a conversation with my best friend, for god's sake. "Were you unhappy before this?"

He pauses at the question. I see a glimmer of the old Topher, and it's all I need. I have not lost yet.

"No, of course I was happy." He pauses, lost in his thoughts. I have him, he is nearly there, just need some time alone.

"Um, sorry," his girlfriend says. "But I feel like you are diminishing Topher's intelligence and ability to connect and to transform. Why do you want to stop him from becoming a better him?"

"Because I like who he was just fine, and I'm pretty sure I wasn't talking to you," I snap, my voice ice cold. We stare, locked, looking at each other.

"Elita!" Topher gasps.

The door swings open with dramatic effect, and it can only mean one thing. Lincoln Jones has another trick up his sleeve.

"The time has come." He parades in, stepping up to the table in the middle of the dining area. Smurfs come running around clearing the plates. I panic, not knowing when I will be fed next and shovel more food in my mouth.

The room energies erupt. He has a way of bringing excitement to people, but for me I am not looking forward to anymore of his dangerous trials.

"To really transform. To really excel. You have to be ready to look past your own vanity." Lincoln Jones picks up hair shavers. "It is time for all of us to tear up these tickets."

One of the Smurfs next to him pulls off her wig. She is bald, with only a thin layer of hair that has grown back.

"Who is first? Who is first to tear up the ticket we all have called vanity?"

He is out of his fucking mind if he thinks anyone is going to shave their hair.

Three hands fly up.

What? Are these people insane?

A lady, the first one killed at the beginning of the trip, walks directly to the seat that sits in front of Lincoln Jones. He hands the shaver to a worker and all that you hear is the sound of the shaver as thick black locks of hair fall to the floor.

My mouth open in shock, I turn to Topher and see the same look mirrored on his face. My stomach drops and I look back as I watch a line form. Smurfs approach, herding us like sheep to form a line outside. My feet take me as I follow, walking behind Topher. Lining up for Lincoln Jones to shave my head.

14

The Line

FRIDAY

Even as I try to play the part, my body physically won't let me walk. My feet will not budge, my brain finally telling me, "Stop it. Run. Go home."

A small nudge on my shoulder by a Smurf breaks my shock just as Topher is approaching the front of the line. The adrenaline finally kicking in and it's what my flight or fight mode needs.

I survey my surroundings and a group has formed that have already undergone this new transformation. No questions, no one asking the logic behind it. What has doing this got to do with being an improved you? Fuck, call me vain, I like my hair and I don't want to cut it, let alone shave it.

And not just me. Topher, he spends more time and

money on his hair than his shelf stacking job can afford to pay him.

Another person, this time an adolescent male, stands from the chair. Lincoln Jones has moved from the main shaving stage to take a seat at a table. They bring a beverage with ice to him as he sits waving to the next, who blindly follows his orders.

There is no red tinge to his complexion, I can't see any cracked lips from here or signs of physical exertion from him. The frail bodies in front of me aren't looking so great. There's a slow and steady pace to the movement of the group. From the way they are all sounding, to the rate at how fast they walk. The longer he keep us like this, the more susceptible we are to conform to his world views.

That I'm starting to believe. There is no other reason Topher is still standing and not visibly freaking out.

I need to think of something and only have a couple things on me.

I have had a hunch about Lincoln Jones for a while now. There is no way I believe that the person in front of me is unknown overseas where he is from. Impossible. Nothing online, other than purchasing tickets to his shows in Australia. Something doesn't add up.

He is hiding something. Just like Topher's parents. But just like anyone who is hiding anything, one thing they can't overcome is paranoia. Let's see how big his problem is.

I slip my hand under the hem of my shorts to the little

compartment I sewed into the inside of them. My fingers brush over the Annoy-a-tron, the small device Topher had pranked me with not that long ago.

I know the settings by heart, testing the entire way on the bus. Sitting in the chair with my eyes closed and going over it, I slip it to option three. This one sounds more like a distant drone or helicopter, a frequency that he may or may not hear over the sound of the birds, wind and those offending shavers. But if he does, I might be in for a shot to stop this.

I was planning to use this for the meditation we have scheduled after this, but I have to try it now. There is no fucking way I will be shaving my hair, consequences be damned. But maybe I can stop Topher from doing something I know he will regret.

I flick the other side button to on, setting the device and waiting.

Another woman, I think her name was Maryann, sits on the chair, her eyes petrified and vulnerable, but she sits still and waits.

I turn right before they turn the shaver on; I hear the device go off. A second later the shaver starts. Not one person has shown they heard anything, I look at Lincoln Jones and he is happily nodding to one of his minions in blue. Funny how all of them have their fucking hair.

Shit. Now I have to wait again until it goes off. The random intervals make it hard to predict. I need to plant the idea in his head to be on the lookout.

I turn to face the other direction in the line, a confused face goes to say something, but I just look up to the sky, cover my eyes blocking the sun with my hand and search the clear blue uninterrupted sky for a pretend flying object.

Hey, he likes pretend things. Why not a drone?

"Everything ok?" Lincoln Jones calls out. I pretend I don't think he's talking to me, although there is no one else making a spectacle of herself.

The guy in front of me that's watching dumfounded, politely taps my shoulder. "Hey, he's talking to you," his hushed tone breaks my fake concentration.

"Huh?" I look at him, furrowing my brows. He points to Lincoln and I turn. "Oh, sorry." I shake my head. "I thought I heard something." With a look up to the sky and around my surroundings, I scrunch up my face and look forward again, hoping to stir unsettlement within Lincoln.

Topher is looking at me when I turn. If only I could read his mind and find out how to get through to him.

"Ok, next. Come on." Lincoln Jones stands now, walking closer towards the line, his eyes glancing up and down from the sky. It's working.

A flash of horror falls on Topher's face. "You got this!" his new girlfriend calls out from the sidelines in her blue shirt. My eyes narrow on her, but Topher snaps out of his trance and staggers to the chair.

My stomach's in knots and my eyes are fixed on a boy

I barely recognise. He sits and blankly stares forward.

It is then the sound goes off.

I look up again, making it obvious. In my peripheral, I see Lincoln squint. He heard it; I know he did. He also follows me as I look up. This small bit of information I have planted in his head should feed into his paranoia, if in fact he is hiding something.

His eyes then land on me, and I see it's working. I hold his gaze, my brows furrowed, looking confused as the shavers turn on.

I force my muscles in my face to stay still, my eyes turn to Topher as the shaver approaches. The man holds down the top of his head with one hand, and with the other he places the blades in the middle of Topher's forehead, perched, ready to start.

The sound goes off again.

I throw up my hands, exasperated, looking up.

"Stop!" Lincoln Jones calls out suddenly, his eyes still glancing above, almost ducking, he walks towards the front. "Pack it up. We're late."

The blades resting on Topher's forehead are pulled back.

My body slumps and my heart rate still pounds, but the lump in my throat is no longer threatening to choke me as they turn the shaver off.

Finally, a win.

Topher opens his eyes. Panicked, confused, relieved?

Maybe all of them.

"Get everyone ready for the next session now. Inside." He points to the tin shed.

I want to do a happy dance, but I beeline to Topher as he's walking aimlessly now towards the shed where Lincoln Jones points to his minions.

Before I get close, a hand grabs my arm. I turn, ready to tell whoever to shove it, but Lincoln Jones has a firm hold.

"Come with me." His eyes pin me in my place and I have no other choice but to nod my head.

~

When he stops walking, he lets go of my hand, the camp now out of sight, and we are standing under the shade of the tree where I have hidden my phone behind the large mine site.

I position myself between me and the loose bark where I implanted the mobile, the sun behind me.

"You look like an angel in this light," Lincoln tells me as his fingers brush a loose strand of hair from my eyes.

I want to vomit.

Instead, I garner a small smile. I look down. "Thanks," I say. If only he knew what I want to do to him, he would call me a devil instead. My forced smile turns into a real one at the thought.

He eats this up.

"You really are extraordinarily beautiful." He stands watching me. Normally I'd roll my eyes at such a cheesy pickup line, but I am torn on how to handle this.

If it weren't for Brian, I might use his obvious appreciation for me to my advantage, but I love Brian and won't impede on my relationship. Well, more than the lying I already am doing to him.

"Should I be back with the group? I'm not missing anything, am I?" My meek voice is grating my nerves, I hate sounding this vulnerable, even if this is a role I'm playing.

"In time, Elita. They are just getting warmed up with the guided meditation. You won't miss much."

Guided meditation? Yeah right, I know exactly what that means and I'm in no rush to get my mind controlled, thank you very much.

"Mary says you are here to convince her son to hate her?" he asks.

"Mary has a few screws loose," I blurt out. Then slam my mouth shut. Fuck.

He throws his head back and laughs; I let out an audible sigh. "Ah, the human condition." He shakes his head, looking at me. "You are different, aren't you?" His eyes are glistening.

I shrug. "I don't think I am." I take a small step back from his intimidating presence. Is this what Jeremy means by love bombing? Showering me with compliments? There must be a reason this seems to work with people. Not with me. Somehow, I can smell bullshit and right now Lincoln Jones smells like shit.

"Actually, Mary is right," I say. Time for me to go on the attack.

His eyebrows raise and he cocks his head, his smile fades. "Really?"

"Initially, I was worried about their intentions, about why they would come back now after all this time. After all this silence."

He stands still as he listens.

"I mean, who leaves their only child for all these years? You know?" I shake my head.

He nods.

"Then I came here," I pause and bite my inner lip and look back into his eyes. I force myself to see Brian staring back so I can say this next part with even a drop of sincerity. "And met you. And it all became clear." His smile returns, not beaming but curled to one side. "And it is because of you they saw their errors and are doing what they can to make up for it. So it is you I should thank." I shake my head. "And learn from." I stand, facing him in awe.

"Well, you can go ahead then." He nods to me.

I frown, unsure what he means. He lifts his hand to mine, palm down, and nods to it. "You can thank me now."

He leaves his hand there.

If he wants me to shake it, he could at least give it to me in the right way. Then it hits me. He doesn't mean shaking it.

Bile rises in the back of my throat. He wants me to kiss his damn hand and I don't see a way out of it.

I inhale a calming breath and cradle his extended hand and lifting it to my lips I fight back my gag reflex and press my lips to the back of it. "Thank you," I whisper.

The whole while he watches like a predator. He nods. "It's time to return," his husky voice sends warning signs to my survival instincts.

Something has happened here, I don't know what it is, but I will find a way to use it to my advantage.

Lincoln Jones has secrets, and it's time to find out what they are.

We walk back in silence, straight to the large shed. He opens the door for me and points to an empty spot at the back for me to sit.

No one moves, no one turns. Eyes are closed, some people sitting on the floor, some laying. Topher sits in front with the usual group he now surrounds himself with.

While Lincoln Jones takes his place at the stage. Undetected, I turn the device in my shorts to the fourth setting. The one of crickets. This is the setting I resolved myself to use, something that can be found in nature and nothing that would give it away.

This will be my anchor to my own free will. Every time I hear the cricket, I will focus on the reason I'm here. Topher, and bringing him back home.

The serene background sounds are wafting through the speakers from the stereo system at the front. Lincoln Jones picks up the microphone and I sit turning on the Annoy-A-Tron.

I close my eyes and run through the ABCs, as his voice welcomes everyone to the day of enlightenment.

~

I sway as I start from zero again. The new game I started to play with myself a few hours ago. When I hear the cricket, I count from zero and see how fast and how much I can count in my head before it sounds again. So far my personal best is 805. It's well past lunch, I have lost count of the hours that have gone past. My legs are numb from sitting in the same position and I'm struggling to keep out the ridiculous teachings.

It has been hard to listen to what he's saying so I can get as much information to use against him as possible. But every time I follow, my resolve slips, my body relaxes and I feel a shift in myself. I'm too aware of what's going on.

I've heard enough. The constant implanting of following him, he will lead us, he has been told the truth; he knows how we can unlock our true potential. He knows how we can ascend and truly become immortal.

Now he isn't even in the room. He left hours ago, but his voice is still bellowing out of the speakers.

A tap on my shoulder makes me jump in my seat.

"Oh, I'm sorry," the young man that had brought the luggage in whispers. "But you have to follow me."

Thank god I get to leave. I stand, but my legs give out and my head spins. He catches my arm. "Slowly, I got you." The kind boy helps me out of the hot shed.

Still no one moves as I'm ushered out.

"What's wrong?" my dry throat croaks out.

"Oh nothing, you just have to get ready, we have to head in soon."

"Huh?" I turn my head to him as he guides me towards the underground camping site.

"You have to get dressed for dinner. Lincoln Jones has requested you join him."

"Dinner, where?" My foggy brain's not catching on as quick as I am used to.

"Back in town at the hotel." We walk inside the cave. "He has your dress out for you on your bunk. Be quick, we have to leave in five."

15

The Intel

FRIDAY

The wind blows in my face with the open window. Like a puppy, I'm almost hanging out of the car window. Using its force to wake me up and prepare me for where I'm going.

I shift in the white singlet, short sundress he left out for me. Similar to what Sarah was wearing the first day I saw her but just no flowers.

Malcom, the boy who is driving me to town, doesn't talk the entire car ride. He doesn't even get out when we pull up at the hotel.

"You aren't coming in?" I ask as I'm about to close the door.

"No, I am heading back," he says

I swallow. "Do you know how I'm getting back?"

He shrugs. "Sorry, I don't. I'm sure someone will

bring you." He gives me a kind smile.

Nodding, I close the door and look up to the hotel. So, this is where he's staying. He isn't roughing it, I see. When the car drives off, I fix my bra and shuffle my breasts. The magnet and small bug I placed in there sit uncomfortably.

I don't like that I'm here alone; he's up to something, but I just have to stay alert and look for ways to pry information that will help me convince Topher that he is a wicked man.

When I walk through the hotel doors, I'm hit with the mouth-watering aroma of the boutique restaurant to the left of me. My stomach growls.

"Elita?" A shrill voice calls out.

I turn and groan, Mary is storming towards me.

"What are you doing here?" she hisses.

"Oh, hey." I grin. "This is where you are. I was wondering why I haven't seen you around the retreat. Pleasant hotel," I call her out.

She flushes. "Yes, well, I have already done the retreat." She stands tall and lifts her chin. "I have ascended."

"Well, good for you, Mary." I smile and lock my jaw in place.

She steps closer. "I knew you couldn't handle it. You are too self-involved to do the entire retreat. I will tell Lincoln, don't worry, ok? You can go."

"Go where?" Lincoln walks through the restaurant entrance into the foyer. "Tell me what?" he asks Mary before giving me a once over in my outfit he picked for me.

"Well, did you want to tell him or do you want me to?" she asks me, her voice cocky.

A smile forms on my lips. "I would, but I don't know what you're talking about, Mary." I turn to Lincoln. "Malcolm said you requested me for dinner?" I ask meekly to Lincoln.

"What?" Mary gasps.

I fight back my smile getting bigger. The look on Mary's face is priceless.

"Yes, that's right," he answers but turns to Mary, his face hardening and asks, "Don't you have somewhere to go, Mary?"

She stammers, "I, uh. Yes, I was just going." She holds up a yellow folder.

"Good, so that will be done tonight?" She nods, but her eyes are welling as she looks between the two of us.

"She is wearing white?" she asks, her voice barely audible.

I look down to my dress. Shit, does this mean something? A shiver runs over my back.

"Go Mary, we need that signature tonight," he snaps.

And it's the first time he loses his cool in front of me. Her head drops. He sighs and walks closer, stroking her shoulder. "You have come so far," his voice is low, the same tone that was drilling into us during mediation. He leans closer to her ear. I can't make out what he says and I don't care because when he cups his mouth to whisper, I see the hotel logo on a white card. His room card sticking out from his back pocket.

Adrenaline spikes and after a quick sweep of my surroundings, I step closer and swiftly pluck it from his pocket.

My heart races as I wait to get busted, but it doesn't come. What has come over me? I have never pickpocketed before. My brain must know how dire the situation is. I have nowhere to put the card but behind my back.

I stand motionless.

He pulls back; she looks up, her eyes are lit back up and she smiles wide.

"You two have a nice dinner. Elita, I will see you soon." She walks off.

"Shall we?" Lincoln turns to me and extends his hand for me to go first.

Well, that can't happen. "After you." I bow my head slightly, feeding into his ego. "Sir."

He smiles, leering at me, and leads us into the restaurant.

Triumph swells inside, as I narrow my eyes, focused, following him into the dining room.

He pulls the chair out for me at our table, a bottle of wine already opened.

"Thanks," I say, but he does not move so I can sit. I clumsily move in between him and the chair, being sure to not let him see my back. Unfortunately, this makes me almost flush in front of him, more intimate than I was intending.

"That is a pretty flower in your hair." He softly touches the belladonna lily I put in my hair.

"Thanks." I make sure to place the card on the seat just as I sit down on the chair.

He pushes the chair in. "You have marks on your knees," he adds.

I clear my throat. "I fell the other day, almost down a mine shaft."

"But you didn't." He sits opposite me. "Because everything happens for a reason, Elita. Everything."

He is so full of himself. I smile and nod. "And that is where I found this flower. So again, you are right."

He chuckles and pours wine in my empty glass.

Soon, I tell myself.

Soon this will all be over. I just need to sit and listen to this bullshit a little while longer.

~

"So, you still haven't answered my question." He sips his scotch, moving on from the wine after they packed the plates up after we finished eating. "Something must have happened for you to have torn up your legs like that?"

I cannot stomach this too much longer, enough time

has passed for me to excuse myself.

"I already said it was too dark, and I fell down a mine shaft."

"Why were you away from your camp area we dropped you in?"

I shrug. "You said we were to go on our own adventure."

"Exactly, so you were running from something or to something. Which is it?"

I look down to my wine, really wanting to finish it but not trusting it isn't laced with something.

"That is disappointing," he sighs. I haven't had enough time to go through his room. I know he's trying to play mind games with me, but I need him invested in our dinner a little while longer.

"My mother, apparently." I look up to him.

"Running to, or running from?" he asks.

I think about that, remembering the vision. "I guess from."

"You don't sound too fussed about it."

"Because of you." I smile. That's a lie, but he doesn't need to know that. I'm not fussed because I know I was not in my right mind, nor physical strength to control what happened. So what if she is buried deep in my subconscious? She can stay locked up in the vault in my head for all eternity as long as I don't have to think about it.

And I do not care if that's healthy or not. I'm just

over it.

Well, not according to Brian. Or maybe even Topher, for that matter now. This is what I don't understand; why do people want to go back when the only way we can change is forward?

He leans forward. "Me?" His lips curl in a predatory smile.

"Yes, that night I tore up that ticket." I end it with throwing his own terminology at him. He laps it up and beams.

His phone rings, and he breaks his stare at me to look at the number calling.

Whoever it is seems to be important. His entire body tenses, and he strains when he says, "I need to take this." He goes to stand.

"You stay." I jump up. "I need to go to the ladies' room. Take your time." I nod to the call.

"Good girl," he says to me, jerking me even more. He waves me off as he answers.

I don't wait to hear the phone conversation, even though I would like to know what has him so torn up. I scurry across out of the restaurant. The restrooms are behind the reception area, along with the entry to the hotel suite below, and lifts for the above ground rooms. As I walk, I check the room card. Room 321. What a surprise, a room with a view. The elevator door pings open. As the door closes to take me to the floor level, I note the staircase exit next to the hall where the restrooms are. Unlike the ones from where we are staying, these have custom artwork, lighting and ambiance that screams privilege and luxury.

I reach his room and knock a few times, just in case. When no one answers, I swipe the card and enter. Before I close the door, I take out the magnet and place it near the doorjamb. I have not tested this, so if Jeremy was feeding me horse shit that day, this could all end terribly.

No time to waste, I go systematically through the room as fast as possible, trying to find the best place to plant the listening device.

It's small enough not to be noticed, but bigger than the ones Tony has us normally searching for. This is because Jeremy insists I can access it on my computer from as far as my motel room is.

My eye lands back to the artificial plant on the small coffee table. I pry open the plastic rounded shrub and put the device in the middle, closing the fake leaves around it.

Undetectable.

Now time to get out of here. But I notice an open briefcase, with the same colour file Mary was holding, just by the armchair.

Before I get to it, the hotel door beeps and shudders. Someone is trying to get in.

I freeze.

There's another beep denying entry and the door being pushed again. It worked.

Then starts the knocking, "Lincoln, are you in there?" Sarah asks. What is she doing here? "You promised I could come whenever I needed you," she whines, then tries her card again.

"What in God's name?" she huffs.

I quietly sneak towards the door and peek through the peephole. She gets her phone out, dials, then places it to her ear.

"You promised," she sobs into the call. "You said if I did what you asked, you would be there when I needed." She wipes the tears. "It's been a bad day. I think I'm on the verge of another breakthrough. Please, just one more time," she begs into the phone.

Sarah's words harden my resolve to take this guy down. He's building a group of worshippers, people that look up to him like he is some sort of god, like he said when we first got here.

"But I did," she whines. "I even pretended to lose my grandma's ring like you said to."

My breath hitches. That was I lie? Everything on Jeremy's list is getting checked off. Why? Was it just to deprive me of my lunch or another reason?

"Ok, I'm sorry. You're right. I will get the card fixed now." She ends the call after a while. I would assume Lincoln Jones was on the other end.

I watch until she walks out of the view from the peephole but listen out for the ping of the elevator. Once I hear it, I run back to the chair. There's not much time. I don't want to be here the second time she tries to get in.

Skimming over the files I see one with Topher's name in it. I snatch it and run to the door. Leaning my ear on the door waiting for any noise, and after no immediate senses of danger, I inch it open and peek down the corridor.

All clear.

I run, bypassing the lifts and straight for the staircase, my feet flying down the stairs. The loud beating of my heart sounds in my ear as I breathlessly wait at the exit door on the ground floor. Ever so slightly, I open the door.

The view to the reception desk is blocked from where I am. But there will be a short moment that I will be visible. In that moment all I have is hope that Sarah or Lincoln don't see me.

Closing my eyes and for one last prayer of safety, I take my chances and take off to the restroom.

~

With the documents hidden safely in the hotel ladies' room, I return to the restaurant. There was a reason I did not see Sarah in the lobby when I walked past.

Because she was standing with Lincoln Jones at our table. My body goes rigid, trying all I can to not give up my guilt.

They both turn to me as I approach, my fingers shake so I ball them up by my side. Sarah's face screws up at first, but when Lincoln asks what took me so long in the bathroom, her gasp is obvious and distracting.

Lincoln looks back at me, dismissing Sarah's obvious pain, and waits for my answer. I sift back to our last conversation.

"I was just a bit overwhelmed by our conversation earlier," I say.

This seems to upset Sarah more and she sniffs. "Well, it's fine now, anyway. I have to call this off early." His eyes darting around, his feet shuffling, ready to go. "I have a meeting later." He turns his attention to Sarah. "Take both of you two back to camp in the car."

"But, I thought–" she tries to argue.

"Well, things change. Sarah, try to pull yourself together." He shakes his head and turns back to me. "Don't worry, we can finish this another time," he says and hustles out of the restaurant.

Sarah is talking, but I watch until he walks past the reception desk, not stopping for new cards and to the elevator to go to his room.

Who is he meeting and what's in the file?

I turn to Sarah, her silent tears now spilling down her face. I need to ditch this ditz, and I just thought of the perfect way to do it.

16

The Breakthrough

FRIDAY

I lay her head on the pillow, her body relaxed and one hundred percent asleep. I lump her on the bed, moving her leg so it doesn't hang off.

A few drinks and a tiny pinch of the belladonna later and Sarah was snoring her little head off. I got a bit of information out of her, but mostly she wanted to cry about boys.

It took a half an hour and a quick trip to the restroom to get the file and we left the hotel bar. Sarah had given me the keys, and she fell asleep on the two-minute drive back to the motel.

I cover her with a blanket. Maybe a good night's sleep is exactly what she needs.

With no time to waste, I head straight for my laptop.

I need to connect the computer to the bug to stream the recording.

After a few attempts, the connection becomes stable, and the microphone is now live. That's what it says anyway, so there must be no one in the room.

Damn, did he leave to go to the appointment?

I leave the audio running in the background and turn my attention to Topher's file. The first few pages are the standard checks: Credit, court archives, employment. The deeper I get into the file, the more apparent that his breakthrough techniques to achieve awareness and ascension are not by following his messed up games. But is cleverly designed.

There are sophisticated profiles, pulling information based on social media comments and messages. There's a questionnaire Topher must have had already filled out. Possibly at the weekend seminar he went to. Here he lists all his fears, hopes, weaknesses. His parents must have helped to give the person who put his analysis all together. There are details from his early childhood.

No wonder he can manipulate people so easily. He is playing with a loaded deck and controlling the narrative before Topher even sat down at the table.

There's a yellow, thick envelope, the last thing left in his file. When I open it and read the first paragraph, it all becomes painstakingly clear.

In my hands is the last will of David Gallagher, Topher's grandfather. He is the sole beneficiary of two-hundred and thirty thousand dollars.

My mouth hangs open.

This is life changing. This will give Topher a leg up, a jump start he deserves. He needs to know. Does he know?

The toilet flushes.

My head snaps to the bed in the room. Sarah is still sound asleep. My heart races and I scan my surroundings for a weapon. Then I hear a knock and realise it's coming from the computer.

"Come in," Lincoln Jones says. "Can I get you a drink?" His voice doesn't hold as much confidence as it did at dinner.

I plug in my headphones and turn the volume up.

"What for? Not staying long," a deep voice returns.

I gulp. I don't need to be in the room to know the tension is high. And this guy is someone you don't want to mess around with.

"You're late with the payment," the unknown voice says.

"I know, but–" they cut him off.

"Listen, we are letting you keep up your little fucked up gig you got going here. But don't forget that the payments need to be coming in. You're down two now."

The sounds of grunts and groans fill my ears. "It's getting sorted tonight. I will have it soon. I promise." Lincoln cries out in pain. "I promise, I promise. I have a couple hundred coming to me soon. I will pay three months in advance to make up for it."

A couple hundred? Topher's money. That's what Mary had in her file. That's why he was so adamant to get it done.

"Good, because you don't want to go back to the states, do you, Keith Allen Janssen? Remember what we give we can take away."

I search the internet for that name. A hit. A myriad of results land on the page, headlines ranging from guru charged with manslaughter, three deaths under Guru Keith Allen Janssen.

I don't wait to hear anything else. Jumping off the chair, I grab the keys. I need to stop Topher from making a huge mistake.

~

I stand and scan the groups of people huddled into their own little worshipping sects. Topher is surrounded by his parents, new girlfriend and friends.

I need to get to him, but there is no way I can do that without causing a scene.

Topher spots me, I see his brows frown as he assesses me, confusion masking his face until his attention is taken away by one of his friends.

Before I get to Topher, I need to get to my phone. It wasn't until five minutes into the drive I realised my mistake. I should have called Brian before I left.

There is no way he can deny it now. When I give him Lincoln Jones's actual name, I know that this all will be over. He will be there to back me up, and I can stop Topher from signing the inheritance away.

Slipping behind the major building, I break into a sprint. When I'm out of sight, I run right around the large mine sight to the tree I planted the phone.

Ripping open the bark, I pull it out. Hands shaking, I unlock it. There is a message waiting on the screen. A message from last night.

From Brian:
I don't know how to say this, so I will keep it short. I have had some time to think things over and I don't think I can give you what you want right now. You deserve better than me. I really am sorry, I wish things could be different. Goodbye Elita.

Time stops.

My hands freeze, eyes locked to the words. I read them again. Slowly, the words penetrate my brain.

My mouth waters, the overwhelming urge to be sick hits me full on. Eyes well as my heart races. I read the words again, trying to make sense of them.

"What are you doing?" A distant voice sounds, but when I look up, Lincoln Jones is standing in front of me. He looks down to my hands.

I follow his gaze and see the phone in my hands. I

know I'm caught, but nothing feels real, no feeling. Is this shock?

He snatches the phone from my hand and assesses it.

How can Brian just end things? Is it a joke? Maybe my issues were too much for him? I know he always wanted to know more, but maybe more became too much.

"Oh," relief sounds in his voice. "Did you just sneak a phone in here to keep talking to your boyfriend?" He tilts his head to the side. "Well, ex-boyfriend now."

The tears fall on their own, my eyes still not wanting to blink, hoping they will go away, but they fall down both sides of my face.

Why would he walk away from me? How could he?

"I can help you answer that," Lincoln says, and he walks closer.

Did I say that out loud?

My voice won't work, I shake my head instead. It's the last thing I want to hear, anything out of his mouth.

"Don't you want to know why he left you?" He steps closer. "Do you think it's a coincidence this keeps happening?"

"What?" My voice breaks.

"Shh, it's ok." He rubs both arms now. "He left, didn't he? Just like your mother left you?"

I look up to him now, my heart being ripped open. How did he know that? I don't think I can hold on.

"It isn't their fault, how can they love someone that

doesn't know how to love at all?"

I hiccup as a sob breaks loose. Maybe he is right. How can I expect Brian to stick around when my own mother couldn't?

"That's it, Elita, let it out." His breath is on my ear. "Don't you see you are the reason this happens, you want to be the victim, you aren't loveable because you are stopping yourself."

I close my eyes tight, his words too strong, too raw. He walks to come up behind me.

My strap falls off my shoulder as a hand lands on my thigh, fingers slipping under my dress. "I can help you." His mouth is close to my neck.

I step forward, barely conscious of what is happening, but my body rejects it on its own. His other hand wraps tightly around my waist. "You don't understand what runs through me, I'm going to help you. I will empty my seed in you and you will no longer have this ticket to bear."

Just like that, it breaks the spell. The real danger comes to light, my emotions, and my broken heart, have taken complete control now; I have lost the upper hand.

Worse.

His hand forces my legs open, and his other ripping down the front of the dress. I pull my head forward and with force throw it back.

"Fuck!" he cries when my head collides with his face.

"Get off me!" My voice is back.

When I run, he responds quickly by lunging forward, catching my feet, taking us both to the ground.

I slam the side of my face on the hard dirt ground and cry out in pain. Still too far for anyone to hear us.

"Come back here!" He pulls my legs back. I kick and squirm as his strength overpowers my struggle. "No one refuses me."

He lands on top of me, and fear grips my throat as I try to scream for help but his hand forces my head hard into the dirt.

Every time he gets a secure hold, I try to still fight.

"This is the best thing for you. Stay the fuck still." This time he won. With force, he rips my underwear off. Either by defeat or by the weight of his body on top of me, my body dissolves into the sand. Wanting to retreat, to leave.

Then, with a loud crack, Lincoln Jones's body goes limp and heavy on top of me.

With the help of a jolt of adrenaline, I break free from under him. When I turn, I see Topher.

"What have I done?" He stands with a blood stained large rock.

~

Lincoln Jones lays motionless on the ground, blood seeping from an open wound at the back of his head, his chest still rising and falling.

He's alive.

"Oh my god, oh my god, oh my god." I turn and see Topher sway on his feet.

"It's ok." I rush to him. His hands shake, the rock slips out and hits the ground with a thud.

"I killed him." Topher's chest heaves.

"No, no." I turn his head to face me instead of the body on the ground. "I checked, he's alive. You didn't kill him. You saved me."

His eyes snap into focus, eyes now glazing over. I use a hand to pull up my broken dress, the other I bend and pick up the rock with Topher's prints on it.

He may be alive now, but I'm no doctor. Even though I won't admit that now to him, there could be a chance he might slip away. The gash is deep, and the blood keeps seeping. To be safe, we can't leave it behind.

Calling Brian is out of the picture now. First because he just dumped me and second the cops are the last thing we need.

"I am so sorry, this is all my fault. What did he do to you? You're bleeding!"

I am?

I look down to assess my wounds from my earlier fall down the shaft. They are broken open and my shoulder has more scratches.

"It doesn't matter, we need to get out of here." I grab

his arm for him to follow.

"But–" he hesitates, looking down.

I turn. "Did you sign anything? Did your mum say anything about an inheritance?" I ask.

His eyes go wide. "Yes, I just signed before. Why? I don't know what's happening. Why would he do this to you?"

"Topher, I need you to look at me and just listen, ok?" I say, my voice firm.

He nods.

"Whatever he has told you is a lie. His name is Keith Allen Janssen, and he has charges of murder in the states. He has a file on you, he knows everything about you, and he owes money to some guy that sounds like we don't want to be here when he comes to collect."

I can see the shock turn to realisation. His broken heart from the deceit of what his parents have done slowly sinking in.

"We have to go, come on." I grab his hand again and without another word we run. With me leading the way, we avoid any eyes.

I don't stop, and I hear Topher at my heels. The singing from the group wafts through the air, the loud chants and the group activities still going on.

We get to Sarah's waiting car. I jump in the front seat, turning on the engine. When I hear Topher's car door close, my foot hits the accelerator and we floor it out of there.

I drive fast the whole way back to the main street, Topher on the lookout for anyone following us.

How long will Lincoln Jones be out for? What if he doesn't make it?

When we get to the motel, I stop the car and jump out.

"Where are we? Why are we stopping?" The urgency in Topher's voice is almost childlike.

"I got to pack up my stuff."

"Stuff?"

I ignore him and open the door, Sarah still snoring on the bed.

"What the hell? Is that Sarah?" Topher's mouth opens as his eyes go from Sarah to watching me pack up my equipment.

"You already knew?" he asks. "You were right. You saw it and I didn't."

I swing my bag over my shoulder. "Don't do this to yourself. You didn't have a chance, I told you he had a file on you a mile long, he needed the money. You're a victim, but it was not by chance. He is not who you thought he was."

"I just... I can't," he struggles to find the words.

"Then don't," I say, going to the notepad by the bedside table. I scribble a note for Sarah.

Do not go back to him.

His real name is Keith Allen Janssen
RUN!

I tear the slip and grab the letter opener next to it and stab it in the door.

"Let's go." I open it and Topher follows.

We will need to ditch this car soon, but for now it's our only way out of here. We jump back into the car and I throw it in reverse. The tyres screech as I exit the carpark and hightail it through the main streets following the signs to exit the town.

"I feel like they are right behind us. Go, go!" Topher keeps shifting in his seat, bobbing his head back and forth.

Bright lights turn from a bend in the distance, coming in the opposite direction. The first car I have seen since we turned out of the town.

Even though they are going the wrong way to be chasing us, being in a stolen car, having a potential murder weapon with us, all adds to the anxiety.

I check the speed; I don't want to get pulled over. The way Topher is acting and the state of me physically, it looks like we're running from a house of horrors.

And in some ways, we are.

Heat overcomes my body from the inside. I can hear my heart racing and my hands shake as I start to crash and flashes of what he almost did hit me.

I push it back, I just need to get us safe.

"Ow!" I hiss as a sharp pain comes from the back of my neck. "Fuck!" I lift a hand to touch it and it's hot.

"Whats wrong?" Topher turns to me.

"I don't know, I think I got bit." I move my hair, showing where the mark is on my neck. The tattoo that I try to forget that's there.

Topher leans in to check. "It's red," he says.

It would be, I wince in pain as the heat burns. My eyes water and the headlights in front start to get closer as the car passes. The pain shoots so sharply that I swerve the car off the side of the road. Tyres hit the rocks, and when I hit the brakes, the back swerves out.

We both fly up off the seats, Topher hits his head on the roof.

"Ow!" he cries out.

I take my foot off the pedal, the pain slowly fading.

I just manage to get the car back on the road, missing the front end falling down a small embankment.

"What the hell was that?"

"I don't know." I put my foot back on the accelerator and I don't stop.

The tank gets us far, but we have to stop. The adrenaline has worn off for the both of us, Topher crashing hard not long after we relaxed.

~

Nine long hours later, we get back to the big red door. I don't have the energy to get rid of the car right now, but that is on the to-do list for tomorrow.

"We're home." I gently shake Topher's arm.

He opens his eyes and squints, the morning sun out in full force. "We're home?"

I nod.

My achy body gets out of the car and we both slowly make our way to the front door. It feels like a lifetime ago we were here.

"Oh." I turn back to him as I open the door and walk in. "I didn't tell you. Brian dumped me."

"What?" he yells. "How can you wait nine hours to tell me that?"

And just like that, I have my best friend back.

17

Epilogue

LEO
10 HOURS EARLIER

The screen turns on and the delayed broadcast streams on the encrypted channel. After the opening music finishes, the camera pans to Loretta, the ION news anchor.

I pour a stiff drink and sit back.

Interviews, the worst fucking part of this job. But, my father insisted it's what the Immortalies want. He is naïve enough to think this is going to quell the thirst of The Uprising.

What a joke.

"Immortalies from around the globe, welcome. Tonight, we bring you all the breaking news, world events and analysis of the coming Transit of Venus and what we can expect. But first, we have a rare and ground-breaking interview." Her eyes glisten. She knows ratings will be off the chart tonight. No doubt my enemies watching and waiting.

I down the first glass and pour another.

"As King Leonidas once again starts his preparation for his five-year wait for another transit to pass, he spared us some crucial time to answer our burning questions. Let's not waste time and go straight to the interview."

The feed changes to my office in our realm, where only yesterday we recorded this waste of time interview.

Loretta smiles, her eyes sparkling as I sit. I don't look happy, even by my standards. But why would I? I've been down this road before, many times. All that happens is I spend some much needed time training and brooding in books.

Pathetic.

I down the second drink.

"Thank you for taking the time to answer our questions. I imagine it's truly an exciting time for you?" she says.

I laugh. Not on screen. On screen I smile.

"Yes, it has been nearly 300 years," I say.

"Already? Time has really flown." She looks down to her notepad. "And how are you feeling this time around?" She looks up. "The world has transformed since the last time the prophecy had a chance to come to fruition. What is different this time?"

Absolutely nothing.

"We have better coordinates and are confident we will be in the right place. However, there are no guarantees this next transit will be it. But there is another one not long after, so we will make sure we do what we can to be ready."

"There is a lot riding on it. Do you feel the pressure since The Uprising seem to use your false prophecy to push forward their agenda?"

"It's not my prophecy, I did not make it up." I say to her. "The Oracle at Delphi bestowed her vision and wisdom on me two thousand years ago. And as for The Uprising, they will use anything to push their agenda."

"Well, there are some points. For example, the destruction above the core in our rainforests. They have proven it to be from the direct result of the humans and their destruction of their realm?"

"Yes, that is a concern. But what The Uprising want is power, and to take control of the humans and their realm for their own personal gain. If they truly wanted to solve the problem, they would stop their manipulations of the humans to denounce science over religion and stoke the flames."

"Well, let's go to a new question." She smiles, "One for all the ladies out there. You have been the most eligible Immortalie for your entire reign. Being alone must be hard? Are you looking forward to potentially finding your fated mate?"

That's enough. I turn it off.

What a terrible question We all know I'm still going to be alone after all this. I've waited two millennia for the woman with the mark of the OMNI to come into my life. I have no reason to believe this time will be any different. And hope is not something I hold anymore.

The door swings open to the office in my new home for the next five years.

"Hey, there has been a report we have a feeder in our jurisdiction." Broderick stands at the door.

"We just got here." I shake my head.

"Well, what can I say. Guess trouble follows you." Broderick's smug smirk is begging to be wiped off.

"Is it one of ours?" I hope not.

"Yeah, a front for The Uprising. A New Age cult, pulling in high funds for them. Sources say Milan is running this sect." Broderick, as always, is well informed. As he should be, he's Head of Military.

"Where?"

"Up north. Coober Pedy. Five hundred miles away."

That would be a nine-hour drive, but ten minutes if we waited until the sun sets and go there ourselves.

"You know what, let's test out the new kids." I stand and pluck the jacket from my chair. "Get the humans to pull the car around."

"You don't just want me to wait till sunrise, take care of it quickly?"

I fix the cuff of the jacket as I reply, "Milan needs to know we are in town. And I have some energy to burn."

PENNY KNIGHT

WHERE TO FIND

PENNY KNIGHT

on socials @pennyknightwrites

or

www.pennyknight.com

READ NEXT

THE IMMORTALIES SERIES **BOOK ONE**

Milton Keynes UK
Ingram Content Group UK Ltd.
UKHW030145180324
439604UK00005B/646